"You're One Of A Kind, Maggie Harper. Headstrong Or Not, I Can't Help Myself," Shep Said.

As Maggie lifted her head to meet his descending mouth, something wonderful broke loose in her wildly beating heart. Closing her eyes, she leaned against him.

When his mouth tenderly grazed her parting lips, a sigh rippled from her. It was that dichotomy about Shep that always threw her. He looked like a warrior: big, bruising, hard looking and so very, very powerful. Yet, she was privileged to know this other side of him, too, so it was easy to yield to him completely. With him, she was safe. She knew he would care for her as if she were a priceless and fragile treasure.

Moaning, she slid her arms against his broad, tense shoulders. Maggie wanted him. And as his lips moved in a claiming gesture against hers, she knew that what they'd shared so long ago was alive today. That he wanted her now just as much as he had in the past.

Maybe even

I0974849

Dear Reader,

Welcome in the millennium, and the 20th anniversary of Silhouette, with Silhouette Desire—where you're guaranteed powerful, passionate and provocative love stories that feature rugged heroes and spirited heroines who experience the full emotional intensity of falling in love!

We are happy to announce that the ever-fabulous Annette Broadrick will give us the first MAN OF THE MONTH of the 21st century, *Tall, Dark & Texan*. A highly successful Texas tycoon opens his heart and home to a young woman who's holding a secret. Lindsay McKenna makes a dazzling return to Desire with *The Untamed Hunter,* part of her highly successful MORGAN'S MERCENARIES: THE HUNTERS miniseries. Watch sparks fly when a hard-bitten mercenary is reunited with a spirited doctor—the one woman who got away.

A Texan Comes Courting features another of THE KEEPERS OF TEXAS from Lass Small's miniseries. A cowboy discovers the woman of his dreams—and a shocking revelation. Alexandra Sellers proves a virginal heroine can bring a Casanova to his knees in *Occupation: Casanova*. Desire's themed series THE BRIDAL BID debuts with Amy J. Fetzer's *Going...Going...Wed!* And in *Conveniently His,* Shirley Rogers presents best friends turned lovers in a marriage-of-convenience story.

Each and every month, Silhouette Desire offers you six exhilarating journeys into the seductive world of romance. So start off the new millennium right, by making a commitment to sensual love and treating yourself to all six!

Enjoy!

Joan Marlow Golan
Senior Editor, Silhouette Desire

Please address questions and book requests to:
Silhouette Reader Service
U.S.: 3010 Walden Ave., P.O. Box 1325, Buffalo, NY 14269
Canadian: P.O. Box 609, Fort Erie, Ont. L2A 5X3

The Untamed Hunter
LINDSAY McKENNA

Silhouette® Desire®

Published by Silhouette Books
America's Publisher of Contemporary Romance

If you purchased this book without a cover you should be aware that this book is stolen property. It was reported as "unsold and destroyed" to the publisher, and neither the author nor the publisher has received any payment for this "stripped book."

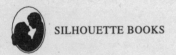 SILHOUETTE BOOKS

ISBN 0-373-76262-3

THE UNTAMED HUNTER

Copyright © 1999 by Lindsay McKenna

All rights reserved. Except for use in any review, the reproduction or utilization of this work in whole or in part in any form by any electronic, mechanical or other means, now known or hereafter invented, including xerography, photocopying and recording, or in any information storage or retrieval system, is forbidden without the written permission of the editorial office, Silhouette Books, 300 East 42nd Street, New York, NY 10017 U.S.A.

All characters in this book have no existence outside the imagination of the author and have no relation whatsoever to anyone bearing the same name or names. They are not even distantly inspired by any individual known or unknown to the author, and all incidents are pure invention.

This edition published by arrangement with Harlequin Books S.A.

® and TM are trademarks of Harlequin Books S.A., used under license. Trademarks indicated with ® are registered in the United States Patent and Trademark Office, the Canadian Trade Marks Office and in other countries.

Visit us at www.romance.net

Printed in U.S.A.

Books by Lindsay McKenna

LINDSAY McKENNA

is a practicing homeopath and emergency medical technician on the Navajo Reservation in Arizona. She comes from an Eastern Cherokee medicine family and is a member of the Wolf Clan. Dividing her energies between alternative medicine and writing, she feels books on and about love are the greatest positive healing force in the world. She lives with her husband, David, at La Casa de Madre Tierra, near Sedona.

To Emile and Patricia Daher,
who serve the best food in Sedona at Shugrue's.
It's a joy to come and relax, laugh and share
pleasantries and friendship.

One

"**Y**ou could die on this mission, Maggie. This one is no walk in the park." Dr. Casey Morrow-Hunter drilled Dr. Maggie Harper with a hard look hoping to convince her of the danger she'd be facing. The world-renowned virologist sat on the other side of Casey's huge oak desk at the Office of Infectious Diseases.

Maggie raised her eyebrows slightly at her boss's huskily spoken warning. Sighing, she lifted her long, artistic looking hands. "I risk my life every day in the hot zone. So what's new?" With a shrug of her shoulders, she gave her a challenging grin. "Tell me *what* in our business *isn't* dangerous, Casey."

"Touché," Casey muttered. She tapped her pencil on the top-secret file that was open on her desk as she studied the woman before her. Maggie's red hair, which was almost always captured in a chignon at the nape of her long neck when she went into the lab to work with deadly viruses and bacteria, flowed across her proud, thin shoulders. Casey had caught Maggie and pulled her into her office for this discussion before the doctor had a chance to suit up for hot zone work scheduled later that morning.

Maggie pulled the tea bag out of her flowery cup and placed it on the white china saucer balanced on her crossed legs. "So," she murmured, giving Casey a knowing look, "what little special assignment have you cooked up for me this time? You know how bored I get. It must be a field assignment? To Africa?"

Casey smiled at her assistant. Maggie was only five foot three inches tall, but she was a firm one hundred and twenty pounds and an all-around athlete. Despite how small she was, Maggie had a seventeen-hand-high Thoroughbred that she raced in cross country events whenever OID issues didn't take her weekends away from her. Twelve miles and twenty or so challenging jumps at top speed didn't faze Casey's friend of many years. Maggie could break her neck at any time. More than once, Casey has seen her limp into the OID after a brutal weekend of competition. And now, at the thought of a new assignment, Maggie's hazel eyes inevitably were sparkling with life. She liked living on the edge.

As if that wasn't enough, Maggie was not only on the OID sharpshooters' team, she was leader of it, being more than a little handy with pistols and rifles. Which was why Casey had pulled her for this dangerous mission. Maggie thrived on competition and adventure. When in danger, she was coolheaded, and didn't allow her emotions to interfere with the steps a doctor on a mission for OID often had to take to save her life. More than once, Casey and Maggie had had a good chuckle over Maggie's trauma-junkie attitude toward life. It served her well in their dangerous field missions to epidemic outbreaks around the world.

Tapping the file, Casey said, "I'd take this one myself, but as you know, I tested positive for pregnancy a week ago."

Glowing with genuine joy, Maggie sipped her tea. "I know. I'm thrilled for you and Reid. Is he still walking on air?"

Chuckling, Casey nodded. "Yes, and he's having hissy fits over me working with all these microbes, saying I've got to be extra careful now."

"Yeah, like in our business, we're sloppy." Maggie burst into laughter.

The room rang with their black humor that only those in the medical field could truly appreciate. Behind Casey through the slats of the venetian blinds, the sun sent blinding light into her pale pink office, drawing her eye momentarily to the peaceful landscape paintings on three of the four walls. "Oh, he's like any expectant father. A worrywart," she murmured softly.

"That's why you took yourself off the hot zone list." Maggie nodded and squeezed a tad of lemon juice into her tea. Delicately, she placed the lemon wedge on the side of the saucer. "Wise move. Have you had morning sickness yet?"

Rolling her eyes, Casey said, "I'm only six weeks along. And no, no morning sickness—yet."

Sitting back in the expensive leather wing chair,

Maggie sighed. "You've got a wonderful guy. But I think you know it."

Casey's eyes grew soft. "Yes, I do. But he knows he's got a wonderful woman, too."

Grinning widely, Maggie said, "With that kind of respect for one another, a marriage is sure to last."

"Humph, unlike these two-to-five-year throwaway marriages I see littering the landscape everywhere I look."

"Well," Maggie said, "those people marry too young. They don't take the time to get to know the other person—or themselves." She grimaced. "I almost made that mistake back in college. I learned my lesson, believe me." She took another sip of tea. "I'd rather be single than make the same mistake twice."

Casey nodded. She knew Maggie had come close to getting married a couple of times in the seven years she'd worked at OID. Both relationships had fizzled. And both times the reason had been that the man wanted to control Maggie, who, being a very modern woman, wasn't about to kowtow to any man. It had to be an equal partnership or she wasn't going to even think about getting involved. Too many men still felt it was their right to tell a woman what to do. Fortunately, Maggie had the grit, the confidence in herself to know better. Still, Casey held out hope for the brilliant, courageous medical doctor. Someone would come along who truly appreciated everything she brought to the table.

"So, what's this dangerous mission?" Maggie inquired.

"This is *really* dangerous, Maggie. It's not like you gallop pell-mell down a steep hill to a four-foot jump, believe me."

Leaning forward, she said, "Tell me more."

Seeing the glint in Maggie's eyes, Casey knew she'd chosen the right person for this mission. "Okay, here's the skinny on it." She flipped open another page of the top secret file. "I got a call from Perseus last Friday. They are a supersecret government entity that works deep behind the scenes with our national security agencies. Morgan Trayhern, the head of Perseus, asked me for a volunteer from OID because there's a bioterrorist group active in the United States right now. Some of Morgan's people just captured one of their top people, a professor who possessed genetically cloned anthrax bacteria. They've found out from this professor that the terrorists are trying to get more anthrax because Morgan's people captured their only supply."

Maggie nodded and finished off her cup of tea. "We have it here, in our lab. The only material known in the U.S.A."

"Right, which is why the spotlight has shifted to the OID." Casey frowned. "Black Dawn isn't a wasted word on you."

"No…it's not." Maggie set the cup and saucer on Casey's large desk. "Don't tell me they're involved in this?"

"Up to the gum stumps," Casey muttered unhappily. "They are the slickest, most professional and dangerous bioterrorist threat in the world today."

"Ouch." Maggie stood up and slid her hands into the pockets of her lab coat. "So, how do we figure into this odd equation?"

"In a very interesting way, believe me," Casey said admiring the tall, proud way Maggie carried herself. There wasn't an ounce of spare fat on her frame.

Maggie was the picture of bravery and steadiness, in Casey's opinion, and she would need all of that—and then some—if she took this mission.

"Morgan is setting a trap for them. Well, several traps, to flush the rest of Black Dawn's operatives in the United States into the open. I've approved his plan. What Morgan needs is a decoy from OID to tip their hand."

"Hmm, sounds fascinating," Maggie said, slowly walking to the windows and looking out through the blinds. Outside the OID building were long, sloping green lawns and huge live oaks. Maggie often looked out to the huge, centuries-old oak trees when faced with a new challenge at work. The sight of the trees comforted her, as they typified the South, where she was born.

"Well, let's see if you continue to think that," Casey said, glancing over her shoulder. She saw Maggie's oval face grow pensive. Even though she was a risk taker of the first order, when things got serious, Maggie could walk her talk. She wasn't irresponsible when the chips were down.

Fingering the file, Casey turned another page. "Here's the plan. Morgan wants to draw Black Dawn out. The only way we can do that is to set up a decoy situation. We know they've lost their genetically altered anthrax, because the FBI found it on Kauai, Hawaii. Black Dawn will want more. Morgan will rig a call that we know Black Dawn has bugged, alerting them to the fact that OID is sending a vial of it north, up to the army base in Virginia. That's where you come in, Maggie. You will be the official courier responsible for getting this vial up there."

"That's really interesting," Maggie said, turning

and studying Casey. "And then Black Dawn will descend upon me to get the vial, right?"

"That's what we're hoping." Opening her hands, she added, "Of course, you'll be well guarded. I don't want you to think we're throwing you out to the terrorists like a bone to a dog."

Chuckling, Maggie walked back and sat down in front of Casey. "I figured as much. So, you need my shooting ability because Black Dawn plays hardball, right?"

"Yes," Casey said unhappily. "I tried to persuade Morgan to send a policewoman, or a woman from the military, but he argued that Black Dawn might not go for the trap because they'd know a member of OID was not involved. We *always* send along one of our virologists with any shipments in transit from OID."

"SOP," Maggie said. "Standard operating procedure."

"Yes." Casey tapped her fingers against the file. "This is going to be *very* dangerous, Maggie. I don't like the plan. I understand it, but I don't have to like it. Putting you in danger is my biggest worry. Black Dawn plays rough. The FBI has promised full cooperation with Perseus on this mission. You'll be well guarded, but that's no guarantee. I told Morgan of my concern over this. They can't just put you in a car with the case containing the vial and tell you to drive from Atlanta to Virginia by yourself. He agreed. So he's sending his top mercenary with you."

"Ah, company," Maggie said with relief. She rolled her eyes. "At least I'll have company on this trip."

"You always have a sense of humor," Casey muttered worriedly.

With a short laugh, Maggie shrugged. "Hey, listen, I've been in some pretty dire circumstances when I ride that wild horse of mine. And I've felt some serious pressure while trying to win a pistol shooting award for OID. Either way, no matter what the stakes, it's pressure. I thrive on it. You know that."

"Well, how's the mission sound so far?"

"Okay," Maggie said. Her hazel eyes narrowed. "Frankly, I'd like to flush some of those bioterrorists out of the woodwork. If I can be of help, I'm volunteering. I'm sure the FBI is going to shadow us."

"They will, but they can't shadow you so close as to scare off Black Dawn. It's going to be dicey, Maggie. They could strike at your hotel room, or when you're driving on the interstate…anywhere. You've got to be on full alert a hundred percent of the time."

"As long as you give me a flak jacket to wear—not that I like those things, they are so uncomfortable—and a Beretta pistol to carry, I'm game."

Drilling her with a searching look, Casey asked, "You're sure about this? You do want to take the mission?"

"Why not? What else am I doing, anyway? I'd like to think my life counts for something, and if I can help bag the bad guys, that will make me feel like I'm doing something worthwhile for humanity."

"You've got a big heart, Maggie. I don't know about your logic, though," Casey said, scratching her brow nervously.

Reaching across the desk, Maggie shook her finger at Casey, "Listen, big mama hen in the sky, I'll be fine! I'm an OID sharpshooter, remember? Our team is number three in the U.S. We've got a shot—pardon the pun—at the next Olympics. I intend to keep leading the team. I'd love to try for gold.''

Grudgingly, Casey nodded, ''I think you're a twenty-year-old inside that thirty-six-year-old body.''

Laughing heartily, Maggie got up. She was never one to stay still for long. Circling the office, hands stuffed into the pockets of her lab coat, she chuckled. ''I'm a big kid at heart. And okay, so I take a lot of chances riding my horse in those events. I know what I'm doing, Casey. I'm *good* at what I do.'' She turned and looked at her supervisor, who was more like a big sister to her. ''I'm right for this mission and you know it or you wouldn't have asked me to volunteer for it.'' With a shrug, she said, ''Besides, I don't have a family. I'm single. No kids. I'm the perfect person for it.''

Turning another page in the file, Casey nodded. ''You're right,'' she conceded. ''Morgan was hoping you'd take it. Black Dawn knows who our best virologists are. You're listed as number three here at OID. That's as good as it gets. If Black Dawn knows you're the courier, Morgan is sure they'll make a play to capture you and the anthrax vial. There's no question in his mind.''

''For once,'' Maggie said, ''my list of credentials will really impress someone.''

With a sour grin, Casey joined in with her laughter. Maggie had graduated from Harvard University at the head of her class. She'd brought millions of dollars in grant money with her when she decided to make the OID her home. In the world of virology, Maggie had more than made her mark. She was known around the world for her abilities and for her pioneering work in the field.

"Well, now that you've decided to take the mission, this is your escort." Casey handed over an eight-by-ten color photo of a man. "He's one of the top mercs at Perseus. A specialist in undercover work."

Still smiling, Maggie reached out and took the photo. When she turned it around, she gasped. The photo tumbled out of her hand.

Casey saw Maggie blanch. "What is it?" She watched as the photo fluttered from Maggie's frozen fingers to the carpeted floor, saw Maggie's eyes widen with shock and then pain. Automatically, Casey got up and moved around the desk. She picked up the photo. As she stood to her full height and her gaze locked on Maggie's, she saw tears in her friend's eyes. But just for a moment. The tears quickly disappeared and Casey saw anger in those hazel eyes, instead.

"What's going on, Maggie?" She held the photo out to her.

"Oh, Lord," Maggie croaked. She took a step away from Casey and the proffered photo. "You aren't serious, are you?" She jabbed a finger at the photo. "Do you know who that is? Do you have *any* idea?"

Nonplussed, Casey looked helplessly at the photo. "Well, yes...Shep Hunter. He's Reid's older brother."

A strangled sound issued from Maggie's throat. She wheeled away and moved over to the windows. Jamming her hands into her pockets once more, she muttered defiantly, "Get that bastard's photo out of here, Casey. I want *nothing* to do with him! Not a damned thing!"

The obvious hurt, the trembling in her voice, shook

Casey. She took a look at the photo once more and then studied Maggie's drawn profile. Maggie had compressed her full lips into a hard, thin line and suffering was written on every square inch of her features. "Maggie, I'm sorry. I didn't mean to shock you. I know you told me that you'd known Shep a long time ago…" Casey grimaced. "I guess there's a lot more to this than you'd told me before?"

Turning coldly, Maggie stared at her across the office, the tension thick. "You could say that." She saw the shock and concern on Casey's face. It was obvious she didn't realize what was going on. "I knew Shep a long time ago," she said in a whisper. "At Harvard. He was going for a degree in engineering. He was a member of ROTC, which led him eventually into the Air Force, to become a pilot." She waved her hand in irritation. "But that was *after* us. After a relationship that lasted my entire freshman year there at the university."

"Oww," Casey murmured, beginning to understand. "So, you two had an affair?"

Her shoulders had drawn up in sizzling tension, and Maggie forced herself to try and relax. Her heart was pounding wildly in her breast. She couldn't control her breathing yet. It hurt to think of Shep. It hurt to remember. Their relationship had ended so many years ago. How was it he could still affect her like this now? With a groan, Maggie turned to Casey. She deserved the full story.

"It was more than that. We fought like cats and dogs, Casey. He wanted to control me. I fought him every inch of the way. We were both independent types. Both bullheaded as hell. He always thought his way was best and my ideas were second best to his.

We fought…brother, did we fight. Of course, making up was a lot of fun, too.…'' She sighed, some of the anger in her voice dissolving. "I've never been in such a wildly passionate relationship before or since. He was everything I'd ever dreamed of in a man, but he treated me like an idiot with no brains. He never thought I had an *equal* idea to his, much less a *better* one. Of course,'' she fumed, "more times than not, my ideas *were* better than his. But he had so much damned pride he'd never admit it. And on top of that, he was the strong, silent type.''

Casey groaned. "Oh, one of those Neanderthal throwbacks, eh? Pride *is* a problem with the Hunter men, from where I stand.''

"He was so arrogant,'' Maggie said, a hard-edged rasp in her voice. "So full of himself. He always thought he was smarter than everyone else. Maybe he was, over in the engineering department, where he pulled straight A's and was on the dean's list. But in my world, he couldn't shed that egotism and arrogance, Casey. He could never relax with me, let go and just be an ordinary human being who had good days and bad days, who *needed* someone else. He was such an iconoclast! He reminded me of Mount Everest—always proud, unapproachable, needing no one and nothing.''

Casey moved over to her side after placing the photo back into the file. "So you broke up because he couldn't really be intimate with you? Is that the bottom line?''

Miserably, Maggie nodded. "Yeah, Case, it was.'' She wiped her eyes. "Damn him. After all these years, I still feel so much for him! My heart is stupid. My head knows better now.'' She pursed her lips and glared out the venetian blinds. ''If he could have said 'I need you' just *once,* Case, I'd have jumped up and down for joy. But he never did.''

''Did you need him?''

''Sure I did,'' she said bitterly. ''Oh, he liked that. He wanted to feel needed by the weaker sex. Well, weak nothing! I was his equal. And he knew it. And he would never acknowledge that. He treated me like a twit.''

''Ouch,'' Casey murmured. ''Neanderthals have that proclivity, don't they?''

Maggie raised an eyebrow. ''You ought to know. You married one of them. But I can't really believe Reid is like Shep. You wouldn't have married him if he was.''

Casey chuckled. ''You're right. I'd have told him to get lost.''

''Maybe Reid's different because he's the youngest of the four,'' Maggie said in a hurt voice. ''He must be. I mean, I've met a lot of men in my life, and Shep Hunter takes the cake for the glacial Neanderthal type, believe me.''

''I met him,'' Casey said slowly, ''about six months ago. He was coming off a mission for Perseus, and he dropped by to see us here in Atlanta.''

Maggie peered up at her. ''And he hasn't changed one bit, has he?''

Hearing the hurt and pain in her voice, Casey shrugged. ''He *tried* to be friendly when he met me. I could tell he was making an effort.''

''Maybe life's changed him a little, after all,'' Maggie whispered. ''With age comes maturity, right? Don't answer that.''

Casey stood there, in a quandary. ''Maggie, if you

take this mission, you take Shep, too. It's a done deal. Everything is set up. Morgan feels that Shep will give you the best chance of surviving.''

Bitterly, Maggie folded her arms against her chest. ''Yes, that's one thing Shep Hunter is very good at— survival. He won't let you into his heart, that's for sure. He'd just as soon walk away from a woman who loved him, really loved him. He's a coward, Casey. Such a coward…''

''Men who can't be intimate are scared,'' Casey agreed softly. ''It takes a lot of courage to share our feelings with one another.''

''Women do it at the drop of a hat. You can't tell me men can't. It's just that they *won't*. That's a big difference. They're made just like us. They have hearts that feel.'' Making a strangled sound once more, Maggie turned and said, ''Don't get me started on this. I used to have this argument every day with Shep. I'm surprised our relationship lasted a full year before we agreed, mutually, to walk away from one another.''

Casey could see the pain in Maggie's large hazel eyes. ''You walked away because it was destroying you. I'm sure Shep walked away out of relief because he couldn't take the pressure of your demands for him to open up and be emotionally accessible to you.''

''You should have been a shrink, Case. Yes, that's hitting the nail on the head.''

''Well,'' Casey murmured, looking back at her desk, where the file lay, ''what are we going to do? I won't be able to change your guard dog for you.''

''I don't *want* him on this mission, Casey. Any-body but him. Please…''

Casey studied her friend's strained features, wishing it wasn't too late to grant her desperate request.

"Well, Shep, what do you think?" Morgan tried to gird himself for Hunter's reaction to the mission. More than anyone in his organization, Shep Hunter was a loner. Morgan knew why and understood Shep's demand for solo missions. Morgan studied the man standing before his desk in the war room of Perseus, which was hidden deep in the Rocky Mountains of Montana. Shep was a giant at six foot six inches tall, and the thirty-eight-year-old ex-air force pilot was one of Morgan's best mercenaries. Shep was heavy-boned and muscular, and even dressed in jeans, cowboy boots and a denim long-sleeved shirt with the cuffs rolled up to his elbows, he looked dangerous. Maybe it was his square face and that jutting, rock-solid jaw that gave Shep such a hard look, Morgan thought. With his short black hair and thick, black eyebrows, which emphasized his frosty blue eyes, Shep Hunter reminded Morgan of a mighty eagle ready to swoop in an attack and gut the quarry he had his sights on.

"Humph," Shep said as he sat down in the chair across from Morgan's desk and continued to read the mission proposal rapidly. "OID, huh?"

"Read on…there's more to this," Morgan warned him briskly. He was prepared to see Shep refuse the mission once he read page two, which identified the OID virologist who would be on the mission with him. Every time Morgan tried to pair Shep up with a partner, he'd refused. They'd had hellacious shouting matches over the subject from time to time, in this very room. And Morgan knew Shep would walk out and quit rather than be assigned a partner. No, ever since Sarah had died on that fateful mission with him, Shep had closed up tighter than an proverbial clam. He absolutely refused to be partnered up again.

And yet, as he tried to appear at ease as Shep devoured the mission brief, Morgan gathered his argument points as to why, if Shep wanted this mission, the OID decoy must be part of it. He just hoped Shep would take it. No one was better suited for this task than Shep, Morgan knew.

Glancing at the photos of his family on one side of his desk, Morgan felt some of his tension easing. The fraternal twins in Laura's lap were smiling. How simple and beautiful life could be. He loved his wife and four children more than anything in the world. Looking up at Shep once more, Morgan realized he saw a lot of his former self in him. Morgan had once been as hard and icy as this merc sitting in front of him. It would take a woman who had metal, who had courage to probe the depths of Shep's fear of intimacy, to help open him up. Morgan acknowledged even today that Laura had had more courage than he'd ever had back then. She'd taken him on—and won. But Morgan was the real winner as far as he was concerned.

When Shep rapidly flipped the page, Morgan steeled himself.

"I'll be damned."

Morgan leaned forward in the chair and put his elbows on his desk. He saw surprise in Shep's normally hard, unreadable features. "What?" he asked tentatively.

"I'll be damned. I don't believe this," he said in a deep tone. He held the file pointing to the photo.

"This is the woman I'm supposed to guard? Dr. Maggie Harper? Are you sure?"

Puzzled by Shep's unexpected reaction, Morgan said, "Yes. Why? Is there a problem?"

With a shake of his head, Shep uncoiled to his full height. Tossing the folder on Morgan's desk, he turned and walked around the large, silent room with his hands on his hips. "I'll be go-to-hell, Morgan. Life really is full of surprises and twists."

Morgan scooped up the file and looked at the photo of the doctor. He didn't understand Shep's reaction. He'd never seen Shep act this way about a mission. And Morgan wasn't sure if Hunter's response was a good or bad one. Usually, Shep would throw the file at him and tell him to go to hell if there was a partner involved. This time, the man's face was softening. Morgan could see a glimmer of something warm and tentative in his icy blue eyes. And his mouth, usually a thin line, had the corners turned up in a slight smile.

Stymied, Morgan held up the file. "Clue me in, will you, Hunter?"

Turning, Shep gave his boss a measured look. Though his fingers were draped casually across his narrow hips, tension thrummed through him. He felt his heart beating hard in his chest. And he felt happiness threading through him. The feeling was completely unexpected, but beautiful. It made him breathe in deeply—as if he were coming alive after a long, long sleep. How long had it been since he'd felt *anything?* Especially happiness? Oh, he'd felt happy for his younger brother, Reid, when he finally met Casey Morrow. And he was overjoyed that Ty and Dev had finally found women they wanted to spend their lives with, too. Yes, everyone in the family was married

now—except him. And each time he'd met the
woman one of his younger brothers had chosen to
marry, he'd felt sad, too. Sad because he knew no one
would want him. He was one mean son of a bitch
who didn't give an inch in a relationship. But after
what had happened to him, how could he?

That was life, Shep decided. Life had been cruel to
him. And torturous. After Sarah... He quickly
snapped his mind shut, like a bear trap. Pain suddenly
intermingled with the quiet joy pumping through him
with each powerful beat of his heart.

"That *is* Maggie Harper?" he demanded. "She is
a graduate of Harvard Medical School, right?"

Floundering because Shep never reacted this way
to a potential partner, Morgan quickly flipped to the
back page of the mission folder and glanced at her
bio. "Yes, Harvard." Looking up, he narrowed his
eyes. "Just what is going on here, Shep? Tell me
what I don't know. Usually you blow up when there's
a partner even mentioned. This time you're standing
over there like a raccoon grinning over a crawdad you
just caught."

Shep smiled a little more widely. "Maggie Harper
was my first real relationship. We met in our freshman year at Harvard. What a hellion she was." He
shook his head in fond remembrance. "She had guts
to take me on."

Tentatively, Morgan murmured, "I see...."

Allowing his hands to slip from his hips, Shep
moved back toward the desk where Morgan still stood
with a confused look on his face. "I'll take the mission, Morgan."

Stunned, Morgan held the younger man's stare.
Shep wasn't one to smile often. He wasn't exactly

smiling now, but the corners of his broad, generous mouth were pulled slightly upward. Morgan saw something else in Hunter's eyes that he'd never seen before: happiness. And hope. He stared back at the color photo of Maggie Harper.

"Does she…I mean, have you had contact with Dr. Harper—"

Chuckling, Shep said, "Nope, haven't seen her in—let's see—almost twenty years. I think I'm going to find this interesting, Morgan. It says she's on a sharpshooting team. Third best in the U.S. She hasn't changed at all. She was riding eventing horses before she went to Harvard. Looks like she's still doing the same thing—taking risks."

"Well," Morgan began, completely shocked by Shep's behavior and his agreement to take the mission, "it's yours, then."

Rubbing his hands together, Shep said, "And I can hardly wait to meet Maggie again. This is going to be some homecoming.…"

Two

Maggie rubbed her long fingers together. They were ice cold. They got that way when she was nervous. She stood in her office at OID, waiting. According to Casey, Shep Hunter would arrive at 0900, and after Casey talked to him, Maggie would be buzzed on her desk monitor to come to Casey's office for a wrap-up on the final details of the mission.

Why, oh why, had she agreed to take the mission? In her angst, Maggie paced the length of her rectangular office, jamming her cold hands into the pockets of her white lab coat. Outside, the day was beautiful. The bright sun and dark green grass and lush trees made her yearn to be astride her Thoroughbred and galloping through the countryside. The sky was so blue it almost made her squint as she looked out the venetian blinds. Her heart and mind swung back to Shep. What a fiery relationship they'd had, each of them bullheaded, each so very sure their own way was the right way.

Maggie ran her fingers through her hair, which she wore loose today because she wasn't going to be working in the lab. No, today was going to be spent arranging details for a very dangerous mission. Maggie told herself she had agreed to the mission because she understood the impact of anthrax bacteria being dropped by bioterrorists on some unsuspecting city. She couldn't stand to think she would refuse a mission because the man working with her was an old boyfriend. Actually, Shep had been much, much more than that. Maggie had fallen helplessly in love with him all those years ago. He'd been a star football player while keeping his straight A average at Harvard. He was keenly intelligent, competitive, and he'd loved her with a passion that Maggie had never experienced since.

Sighing, she ran her chilled fingers through her shoulder-length hair once more. "What have you done, Maggie?" she whispered through tight lips as she ruthlessly perused her desk, which looked like a tornado had hit it. Restlessly, she picked up some papers and tried to concentrate on them.

The phone on her desk buzzed. She jumped. The paper fluttered out of her fingers and wafted to the tile floor.

"Oh!" Maggie whispered, scooping up the letters. She was jumpier than a kangaroo. Her heart was throbbing at the base of her throat. She knew it was Casey buzzing her. It was time. Reluctantly reaching for the phone, Maggie wished she was anywhere but ere right now. She was actually afraid to meet Shep ce again. Gulping, she picked up the phone.

"Maggie?" Casey asked.

"Yes?"

"It's time. Come on down so I can give you two the final briefing on this mission."

Shutting her eyes, Maggie whispered, "Okay...I'll be right there...."

Placing the phone gently back into the cradle, Maggie tried to steady her breathing. It had been so long since she'd seen Shep. Had he changed? Had life softened him at all? Was he more inclined to listen to other people now? Or was he still arrogant and self-righteous? A chill swept through her. She felt fear—raw, unbridled fear. Chastising herself mentally, Maggie automatically touched her hair. Taking a look in the ornate, gold-framed mirror that hung in her office, she saw that her eyes looked huge. Like a rabbit about to face a starving wolf.

Her fingers were so cold they almost felt numb. She was unhappy with her reaction. She was acting like the freshman she'd been when she first met Shep. Back then, Shep always seemed to have the world by the tail. It was as if he knew what would happen next, planned for it and then executed it so easily that Maggie felt like an idiot in comparison. Hunter was always calm, cool and collected. Right now, as she swung out her door and into the highly polished hall that lead to Casey's corner office, she felt disheveled, unprepared and scared.

Giving herself a stern talking to as she slowly walked down the hallway, she greeted her lab cohorts who passed, feeling comforted by the sight of familiar faces. The people at OID had some of the best minds in the U.S. They were at the vanguard of the attempt to keep people safe from killer bacteria and viruses.

Shep was a virus, Maggie decided with mirth. She was infected by him and hadn't built an immunity to him yet. That was why she felt vulnerable right now. But wouldn't eighteen years be an immunity in itself? Time was supposed to heal everything, wasn't it?

As Maggie reached for the brass doorknob that led to Casey's office, her heart beat hard in her breast and she quickly ran a hand over the maroon slacks she wore beneath her lab coat. Mouth dry, she closed her fingers around the doorknob. Inside that office was Hunter. She felt hunted, all right. Taking a deep breath, Maggie jerked open the door and forced herself to move quickly into the office.

Shep contained his surprise. The woman who walked resolutely through the door into Casey Morrow-Hunter's office was even more beautiful, more poised and more confident than he could recall. Despite her small stature, Maggie carried herself proudly, that small chin of hers leading. The years had been kind to her, Shep realized with pleasure. He rose from his chair at the corner of Casey's desk as Maggie closed the door quietly behind her.

Their eyes met for the first time. Shep felt his heart thud hard, like someone had struck him full force in his chest with a sixteen-pound sledgehammer. He struggled for breath as he studied Maggie's oval face, her high, smooth cheekbones. The freckles across her nose and cheeks—those delicious small copper spots—were still there. He saw her nostrils flare. That was something she'd done when he knew her years earlier—something she'd done when she was afraid. Her eyes widened incredibly. He saw every nuance of every emotion she was feeling in her gaze. The fear was there, the uncertainty, the desire…yes, desire. He knew he hadn't wrongly read what she was feeling. That made him feel good. Damn good.

"How are you?" he said, his voice deep and unruffled. Stepping forward, Shep offered his large hand to her. He saw Maggie recoil. It wasn't so much her posture or any outward shrinking away from him; rather, it was in her jewel-like, hazel eyes.

Forcing herself to lift her hand, Maggie croaked, "Fine…just fine, Shep…." As her fingertips slid into his proffered hand, she was once again reminded how large he was. She felt like a midget in comparison. To her right, she saw Casey stand, a smile affixed to her face but trepidation in her eyes. Maggie knew she had to make this work for Casey's sake and for the OID.

"Your hand is cold," Shep murmured, stepping closer and placing his other over the one he'd held captive. So much was flooding back to him about Maggie. Oh, he'd never forgotten that whenever she was nervous and upright, her hands would turn freezing cold. As he covered her hand with his now, he also remembered how small and delicate and feminine her hands were compared to his huge, hairy paws. Shep strangled the desire to pull Maggie into his arms and hold her. What would she feel like? As warm and fragrant as he recalled? A hint of honeysuckle wafted into his nostrils and he drew the scent deep into his chest. He knew it was Maggie's skin and the delicate perfume she wore. He saw her face turn a dull red as she tried to pull her hand from his.

Panicking, Maggie jerked her hand free from Shep's. She stood there, looking up at him and thinking that life had made him even more ruggedly handsome than before. Those ice-blue eyes of his, so wide and filled with intelligence, now burned with a tender regard for her. His mouth curved in a slight smile of welcome. Hunter rarely smiled. She felt special. She felt enveloped by his intense interest in her as a woman. There was no doubt Shep was all-male. Very male and very dangerous to her wildly thudding heart. Rubbing her hands together, Maggie managed to murmur, "You haven't changed at all, Shep."

The corners of his mouth turned upward even more as he watched Maggie nervously rub her cold fingers together. "Eighteen years has done nothing but make you more beautiful, Maggie." And that was the truth. He remembered the soft, young Maggie of before. This was a woman standing before him, mature and confident. He liked that. He saw her arched red brows dip momentarily in reaction to his compliment.

"Have a seat, you two," Casey invited. She pointed to a second chair at the opposite corner of her desk, gesturing for Maggie to sit there.

Relieved, Maggie sat before she fell down. Just the way Shep perused her—with that raw, naked look that was so male—made her knees go weak. She gripped the arms of the chair, relief sheeting through her. Once more she felt Shep's amiable inspection of her, but she refused to look at him. He was so damned intimidating when he wanted to be! Nervously smoothing her lab coat across her thigh as she crossed her legs, Maggie devoted all her attention to Casey. Shep's sincere words echoed through her head. He thought she looked beautiful. Maggie wasn't any cover model, that was for sure. She felt attractive, but not beautiful in the way Shep had suggested. Yet she sensed he was being sincere. That explained why her heart was galloping away within her breast.

People who knew Shep Hunter were often repelled by his glacier look, but Maggie knew the real Shep. Having gone with him for a year, she knew his expression was a façade to purposely intimidate others. He was afraid of being hurt, so he threw up this nearly impregnable don't-even-approach-me kind of demeanor. It worked on everyone except her. She had gotten inside Shep's considerable armor once. She knew the sensitive man who hid behind it, but his ego made him unapproachable. As she sat rigidly in the chair, her hands clasped, she wondered if Shep had kept his sensitivity. Or had life robbed him of that, too?

Maggie painfully remembered that when they broke up, Shep had left Harvard. He'd managed to get an appointment to the Air Force Academy, instead. She knew why: he couldn't stand being at the same school with her. The pain of their breakup had been too much for him to deal with. Stealing a look out of the corner of her eye, Maggie marveled at how wonderful Shep looked. He was dressed in a pair of dark blue chinos, a white, short-sleeved shirt and a pair of jogging shoes—very California-looking compared to the more businesslike dress of the East Coast inhabitants at OID. He was deeply bronzed and obviously spent a lot of time out in the sun. His hair was still ebony with blue highlights, the short length and neat cut shouting of his military background. But it was the thick, black hair on his lower arms and the tufts of hair peeking out the top of his shirt that shouted of his masculinity.

Shep was still in superb athletic condition, Maggie realized. He had always been strong and sturdy. She recalled his football days, and decided he looked just as firm and fit now. She wouldn't be surprised if he regularly worked out with heavy weights at a gym. Her mind continued to wander as Casey riffled through a number of papers on her desk. Was Shep still in the Air Force? Maggie had heard he'd become a pilot of some of the hottest fighter jets available. Was he married? She didn't see a gold band on his left hand, but that didn't mean anything. He could be living with someone. A twinge of jealousy shot through her. Surprised at her emotional reaction, Maggie felt very unhappy with herself. Why couldn't eighteen years erase what Shep had meant to her?

"Okay, here we go," Casey murmured, giving them both an apologetic look. Lifting out the mission brief, she said, "Morgan e-mailed this to me last night over a secure line. He wants you two to pretend that you're a married couple from Atlanta going on a minivacation to Savannah. You will stay there, at a bed and breakfast near the heart of the city, and then, the next morning, continue your automobile journey to Hilton Head Island in South Carolina. You will stay at a time-share overnight, and the next morning continue on to Charleston. From there, you will go due north to Fairfax, Virginia, and the USAMRID facility. The reason he's outlined his route is that it will make the best use of FBI help and protection. The roads you'll be traveling are all interstate and therefore, easier to drive and easier for them to get to you if something goes down."

Maggie opened her mouth and then shut it, realizing Casey wasn't done as she continued to read from the document.

"Again, you are to pose as husband and wife. Morgan will leak out the entire scenario to Black Dawn one hour after you leave here. Black Dawn will know you are couriers in disguise. These routes will give them ample opportunity to strike at you. Morgan has given them your itinerary, route and time of arrival at these places. There will be satellite fly-bys to keep tabs on your vehicle. Each time the satellite orbits the earth, it will make a check on your location. You'll drive an unassuming dark blue Sedan. Nothing fancy. He wants you to blend in and look like tourists on a vacation.''

Casey flipped the page. "Maggie, you will carry the aluminum suitcase, which is small and portable. It will contain the fake anthrax. The vial will be marked to make Black Dawn think it is the real thing, but it's not. But they won't know that they have nothing until they test it out for three days in a petrie dish.''

"Let Black Dawn get close to that suitcase.'' Shep growled. He glanced over at Maggie. Did she know how very dangerous this mission really was? The thought of bullets ripping into her flesh made his stomach contract with agony.

Maggie nodded. "I'll hand it over when the moment arrives, don't worry,'' she muttered. Just meeting Shep's gaze sent her heart skittering. Why did he have to be so good-looking in his rough kind of way? He was no male cover model, that was for sure. The crow's feet at the corners of his eyes attested to years spent living under harsh conditions. The slash marks at the sides of his mouth were deep with time—and the result of too little smiling. His prominent nose had obviously been broken several times. Maybe it was the squareness of his face and that granite chin that made him look like the untamed Rocky Mountains where he'd grown up. She knew he'd probably shaved in preparation for the meeting, but even now the shadow of returning growth gave him a decidedly dangerous countenance.

Casey nodded and flipped the page. "You will both wear flak jackets beneath your civilian clothing. You'll get Beretta 9 mm pistols to carry on your person. The car will have bulletproof windows."

"But not bulletproof metal?"

"No," Casey said. "They're doing what they can to protect you, but this is no armored car."

Shep nodded. "I'll do the driving."

"No, I will." Maggie straightened up, her anger surfacing. "I'm the courier. You're the guard dog. Remember?"

Casey held up her hands. "I think there will be plenty of driving for both of you. This is going to take all your attention, your concentration. Each of you can drive for a couple of hours and then switch off. It will keep you fresh and alert."

Maggie bristled. How like Shep to just walk in and take over. He was beginning to treat her like that little freshman he knew so long ago. Well, she'd grown up. She was damned if he was going to start making decisions without consulting her first! Glaring across the space at him, she saw him scowl. Too bad. He was going to find out that she wasn't the weak little girl he'd met back at Harvard.

"Please understand," Casey said, looking at Maggie, "that just because the FBI is working with us doesn't mean they can protect you twenty-four hours a day. They are human. And so are you. There will be surveillance, but technically, you two are on your own. The cell phone has an emergency number you can dial if they attack. It may take fifteen to thirty minutes to get to you if something happens, depending upon your position when an attack takes place. The FBI can't tail you or Black Dawn will pick up on the fact. They will be stationed at certain points along the interstate, on alert, if you do need help. That's the best we can do.''

Maggie squirmed. ''I understand that, Casey. But why have us married? Why can't we have separate rooms?''

''Because,'' she said patiently, ''Morgan wants Black Dawn to think we're stupid enough to use such a ruse. We want them to think we're inept.''

The news that she would be staying in the same room with Shep was a shock to Maggie. She'd never fathomed such a thing happening. It was simply too much for her to imagine. ''But,'' she protested, opening her hands in appeal, ''I don't see the wisdom of it.''

''There's safety in numbers,'' Shep said as he met and held her widening hazel gaze. His conscience pricked at him. It was obvious Maggie wanted nothing to do with him. Her file said she was single, but it didn't give him a wealth of information about her private life. Maybe she was living with a man? That thought didn't set well with him. Silently chiding himself, he realized he was still just as protective about her now as he had been then!

''Safe?'' Maggie's voice was laced with sarcasm. ''There's nothing 'safe' about you, Hunter.''

His mouth worked and a corner lifted. ''That was a long time ago, Maggie. I think I can control myself for your benefit.''

Flushing deeply, Maggie refused to look at him or

Casey. She was making a fool out of herself and was old enough to know better. Knitting her fingers together, she said in a raspy tone, "I *still* don't think it's a good idea to stay together in the same room. If we had separate rooms next to one another, we'd at least have a chance if Black Dawn tries to blow us away. It would make it harder for them to get to the two of us."

Casey nodded. "That's the point. We want to make it *easy* for Black Dawn to get to you."

Chagrined, Maggie saw the simplicity of Morgan's plan. "I see...."

Casey stood. "Here is your wedding band set."

Stunned, Maggie took the box. Casey went over and gave Shep one. Opening hers, Maggie saw it contained a gold band and a solitaire engagement ring.

"Don't worry," Casey said with a laugh as she stood between them, "it's all fake. Plate gold and zircons, Maggie."

"At least we don't have to stand in front of a preacher," she groused as she studied the bands.

Shep rose easily. "Here, let me put them on you, Maggie."

Casey smiled down at Maggie. "Great idea."

Stunned, Maggie watched Shep approach. "No thanks, I can do this myself." She quickly shoved the rings on the proper finger. There was no way she wanted Shep to touch her. Already her flesh was begging for his touch. Would it be the same as she recalled? Better? Worse? Why did he have to move with such a boneless grace? For all his size, he reminded her of a lithe African leopard. She saw the disappointment in his eyes as she refused his help.

Well, he'd better get used to it. She had a mind of her own and he might as well learn that now.

Shep stood watching Maggie. Her cheeks were stained a bright red as she jammed the rings on her hand. It occurred to him that he'd never met another woman even remotely like her. He felt an old ache from a wound that still scored his heart from their breakup. Only flying his jet, when he was in the Air Force, would assuage some of the loss he'd felt when they'd parted. But it had been a necessary parting. He and Maggie never saw eye to eye on anything.

Looking down at her, he met her challenging gaze. "Casey suggested we have lunch, go over the details and then start the mission tomorrow morning. How about it?" He saw her thin brows draw downward in protest and knew nothing had changed between them. She was nervously fingering the fake wedding ring set on her left hand, as if it were a germ infecting her. As if giving in to him on any point would kill her.

"Oh...all right. There's a cafeteria in the basement. We can go there." She looked at her watch. It was only nine-thirty. "Besides, it will be practically deserted now."

"I had a nicer place in mind," Shep said.

Rising smartly, Maggie glanced at Casey and then drilled him with a look. "The cafeteria is fine. This isn't pleasure, Shep. It's business. I want it kept that way."

The warning growl in her voice made his gut clench. Did she hate him that much? Distaste was clearly written in her expression. But Shep thought he saw fear edging her gaze as she moved robotically toward the door. She kept rubbing her left hand against her lab smock. Fear of him? Why? He had a helluva lot of questions and no answers.

Following Maggie out into the hall, he told Casey they'd be back later. In his hand, he carried a black leather briefcase. As Maggie walked briskly ahead of him, a number of people said hello to her. He watched her face thaw as she cheerfully engaged them in conversation. Damn. This was going to be hell, he told himself as he entered the elevator with her.

Maggie punched the basement button and then made sure she stood opposite Shep. He looked very unhappy. Clasping her hands, Maggie internally rebelled against the wedding ring set. She kept running the bands around and around on her finger. The elevator felt claustrophobic to her. Shep Hunter filled it with his size, and with the incredible quiet charisma that radiated from him like a thousand glowing suns.

As soon as the doors whooshed open, Maggie strode confidently out of the elevator. Choosing a table and chairs near the window, on one side of the cafeteria, she sat down. Shep sauntered over and placed the briefcase on one of the empty chairs.

"Can I get you some coffee?" he asked. "If I remember right, you like it sweet and blond."

Maggie sat very still. She looked up at him. She saw the struggle in Shep's normally inexpressive face. His voice was low and intimate. Her flesh prickled. Oh, how tender a lover he could be! All that hard invincibility melted away to leave a man with breath-stealing sensitivity in its wake. Maggie found herself aching to be with that man once again. Stymied, and afraid of her own heart, she muttered with defiance, "Yes, coffee would be fine, thank you."

He smiled a little at her petulance. "And if I'm

reading you correctly, a shot of brandy in it to quell your nerves?''

Shutting her eyes, Maggie felt her heart blossoming beneath his gentle cajoling. No, Shep was still the old Shep she knew. Oh, how was she going to survive this? She was more afraid of him than the damned assignment!

Opening her eyes, she fearlessly met the warmth that now filled his blue gaze. ''Right now, a shot of whiskey would be my choice.''

Nodding, he said, ''I think I understand why. I'll be back in a minute.''

Just watching him saunter over to the serving area, Maggie sighed. She was being nasty to him when he didn't deserve it. Yet he seemed to be taking her in stride and not letting her attitude get to him personally.

When Shep arrived back at their table, he held a tray filled with food. He set a cup of coffee in front of Maggie, and then a saucer that contained a huge pecan sticky bun. He placed a second plate, piled high with fluffy scrambled eggs, six slices of bacon, hash browns and grits, on his side of the table.

''I'm not hungry,'' Maggie said, pushing the plate with the sticky bun toward him as he sat down.

''I remember it was your favorite pastry,'' he told her, unruffled, as he settled into the chair. The look on her face was one of puzzlement and heartbreaking sadness. With a one-shouldered shrug, he murmured, ''But look, if you aren't hungry, I'll eat it.''

Not hungry? Maggie was starved for his touch. Even the briefest of ones. But Shep could never know that. ''Thanks…you can have it.''

Scooping up a forkful of the eggs, he gazed across

at Maggie as she wrapped her fingers around her coffee mug. "You still get cold fingers when you're upset."

Nodding, she took a sip of the coffee. "I switched to drinking tea a long time ago, Hunter. Being around you makes me want to have coffee again."

His mouth curved in a slight smile. "So, is this good or bad, Dr. Harper?" he deliberately teased her. For a moment, Shep saw her shoulders, which were gathered with tension, begin to relax slightly.

"Being around you is like a bad cold returning."

"Thank you."

"Only *you* would take that as a compliment, Hunter!"

Chuckling, he spread some strawberry jam on his toast. "You haven't changed at all, Maggie. I was wondering if you had, but I can see you haven't."

"Well," she said under her breath, leaning forward so only he could hear her, "you haven't, either."

Gazing at her was like looking at a delicious dessert to him. "So, where does that leave us?"

"At odds with one another. As usual."

"Eighteen years is a long time, Maggie."

"And it's like a blink of an eye, because you were the same then as you are now."

"Thank you—I think."

"Don't start preening, Hunter, because it wasn't a compliment and you know it."

"How's your coffee? Did I get the right amount of cream and sugar in it?"

Flushing, she refused to meet his gaze. Hands gripping her cup, she looked down at it. "Like I said, nothing has changed."

"We're older, if that helps?"

"Just more stuck in our same old patterns and personalities as far as I'm concerned," Maggie retorted. She saw his gaze thaw considerably. When she realized he really wasn't taking anything she said personally, she was stunned. Back then, he had. They'd fought all the time. Fought and made up. And the making up had been incredibly delicious.

"Maybe," he said. "Life has thrown me a couple of curves. I hope I've learned from them."

She sipped her coffee, feeling rebellious. Hunter always brought out her feistiness. Only he could. She wasn't explosive like this with any other man she'd ever had a relationship with. Only around him. "Whatever the reasons, Shep, you bring out the worst in me. All we did then was fight, and from the looks of it, it's starting up all over again." Her nostrils flared. She hated it when her voice quivered with emotion as it did now.

Shep ate slowly, thinking about how he was going to handle Maggie on this mission. There was much more at stake here than she realized. He had to be the boss on this venture whether she liked it or not. At this moment, he wasn't ready to tell her that. They had a day to get ready. One way or another, Maggie was going to have to bend to his way of doing things. Or else…

Three

――――

"I'll drive," Shep said, heading around the car they would be using. The vehicle was parked in the underground garage of the OID building. The July morning was warm and humid, hinting of the high temperatures and humidity to come in the sultry afternoon hours.

"Hold your horses, Hunter."

He turned, surprised at the warning in Maggie's voice. As she stood near the passenger side of the car, Shep had a tough time keeping his gaze from devouring her, because to him, she looked beautiful in the comfortable khaki slacks and dark blue blouse she wore. The sleeves of the blouse were decorated with a touch of lace, giving her a very feminine look. Beneath the silk of the blouse he knew she wore her flak jacket, mandatory on this mission. He was wearing his beneath his white shirt and sport coat. Already the thing was beginning to chafe him, but he knew the wisdom of wearing it.

"What?" She was looking at him with her eyes narrowed. Shep knew that look. Halting, his hands on the top of the car near the driver's door, he said, "What's the problem?"

"How can you ask?" Maggie demanded. She tried mightily to ignore how handsome he looked this morning. His black hair was damp and gleaming from his recent shower. His jaw was scraped free of the shadow of beard that would inevitably appear in the afternoon hours. His eyes were bloodshot, and she wondered if he'd gotten much sleep last night. She sure hadn't; too much of their tortured and passionate past had kept resurrecting itself before her closed eyes while she lay in bed. "Shep, this is *not* a replay of eighteen years ago. You think you know everything. You think that, as usual, I'm a hothouse violet incapable of being your equal."

"Wait a minute—"

"No," Maggie said coolly, locking her gaze on his frosty one, "it's different this time, Hunter. And *you* are going to have to be a lot more flexible than you were two decades ago. Or else!" She held up the keys to the car and smiled a little. "I'm driving."

"I suppose you've taken evasive driver's training?"

"Yes."

"And terrorist evasive training, as well?"

"I can see the surprise in your eyes right now, Hunter." She gave him a smile that dripped with honey. "Yes. And just in case you ask me when, I'm certified for the next year. I just passed the two courses, for the fifth year in a row."

One corner of his mouth flexed upward. "Maybe you *have* changed," he admitted sourly. "Okay, you drive for two hours, and then we'll trade off in shifts. How's that sound to you?" He decided to concede to her on this point, knowing there would be tougher battles ahead—things he couldn't allow Maggie to do herself, for fear she'd get killed. Like Sarah.

Maggie was pleased that he was thinking in partnership terms right now. "That sounds fair and equitable, Mr. Hunter. Thank you for your consideration." She saw his blue eyes glimmer with unease. And the slight downward movement of his hard mouth made her openly grin in triumph. "Nothing has changed at all with you, Hunter, through all these years. You are the same guy I knew way back when."

"Some things don't change," he agreed grumpily. Shep moved around the rear of the car. As Maggie passed him, their hands brushed. How he ached to really touch her, to be able to slide his fingers knowingly up that smooth, warm flesh. He recalled how wonderful she had felt in his arms as they made torrid love to one another.

Once inside the car Shep forced his mind back to business, taking note of the special equipment in the vehicle. An onboard computer showed the map of the area where they would be driving, including all the rural routes and all the country roads. Georgia was full of country roads, and if they got into trouble, they would have to know which one to take to try and escape their pursuers. There were two different radios, one connected to the state police and the other a direct line to the FBI van, a mobile headquarters that would shadow their journey. After testing each instrument to make sure it was operational, he glanced over at Maggie as she strapped in with a special seat harness and adjusted the mirrors.

"I hate flak jackets," she griped as she scratched beneath her right arm.

Shep nodded and shut the door. "They're necessary." He strapped himself in, turned on the computer and opened a laptop, which was plugged into the car lighter. The laptop was mounted where the glove box should have been and sat on a small movable table in front of him, fitting comfortably above his thighs. "Part of the game we're entering," he warned her, in case she had any thought of ditching it because it was uncomfortable.

Glancing at Maggie once more, he felt his heart beat hard, underscoring how much he still…still cared about her. Nightmarish visions of Sarah's death suddenly filled his mind. Blinking hard, he removed the specter. No, he wouldn't let Maggie meet Sarah's tragic end. It had been his fault that his one and only partner at Perseus had been killed in the line of duty. His fault. Only his. Shep would be damned if Maggie got caught in the line of fire because of him. No, he had to control this mission from the get-go—whether Maggie liked it or not. Her life was at stake. He'd lost one woman he'd loved to a bullet. He wasn't about to lose Maggie, too.

"Everything up and running?" Maggie asked as she switched on the car's engine. The Sedan purred to life.

"Roger that," he said, doing a double-check on their computer map. "I'll give you the directions to get on—"

"Never mind," Maggie said briskly, "I memorized the route to Savannah last night." She proceeded to verbally give him the details of where they were supposed to drive. Their route had been set up by the vigilant FBI, and there would be cars with agents placed along certain milepost markers, where other roads intersected the freeway, so that the FBI could give them help sooner rather than later, if they called for it. The unmarked white van would always be on the freeway, ten miles behind them, to relay such information to the awaiting agents.

She saw his face darken as she reeled off the routes in perfect order. What was the matter with Shep? He should be pleased with her preparation for this mission. Instead, he was looking at her oddly. And he seemed more controlling than she last recalled. Not that Shep had *ever* been Mr. Sharing. Nope, not him. Smiling a little, she put the car in reverse and backed out of the space.

"I take that look to mean I got it right. So, let's go, Colorado Cowboy."

Taken aback by her confidence and aplomb, Shep snapped to the business at hand, though hearing her old nickname for him warmed him unexpectedly. His heart swelled with feelings that he brutally squashed. If anything would put them in danger, it would be a lapse of concentration on his part. It was too easy to look at Maggie and drink her in like a tall, cool liquid. She could always quench his fire, satisfy his needs—every last one of them. In some ways, they'd been made for one another. They fit together in a special way that Shep had never experienced since Maggie. He had loved Sarah but she'd been different in many ways. Sarah didn't have those qualities of self-confidence and inner strength that glowed in Maggie like the sun itself.

As they turned onto the road that led to the OID, a redbrick building on a knoll surrounded with manicured green lawns, Shep automatically began to sweep his eyes from right to left. To him, surveillance was a mental game of sorts: look for the cars, memorize their color, their style and how many occupants in each. If they were being tailed by Black Dawn, this was the only way to sort it out. The Mac laptop was hooked directly into police computers, so they could run license plates. A set of binoculars rested between the two front seats, so he could read the numbers from a safe distance.

"I felt you go into alert mode," Maggie said. She pulled the visor down and put on a pair of gold-framed sunglasses. They brought out the highlights in her hair, which she'd gathered in a chignon at the nape of her neck. Already too warm due to the high humidity that was common in the South for this time of year, she adjusted the air-conditioning.

"Yes, you did." Shep studied her profile. She expertly wove the Sedan into morning rush hour traffic. Maggie had always been a good driver, he recalled from his days with her at Harvard. More memories poured back about her and her family. Her father bred race horses for the major tracks in the United States. He was a speed freak and Maggie had certainly inherited those genes. "Your father still racing horses?"

Chortling, Maggie nodded and said, "Yes, Dad is still trying to breed that Triple Crown winner. And Mom continues to go to her bridge parties every week."

Nodding and continuing to look around Shep

asked, "What about racing sprint cars? Does he still do that? He's pretty old now, I'd think."

Pleased that he remembered so much about her family, Maggie briefly met his thawing blue gaze. When Shep let his guard down—which wasn't often—he was open and approachable. The hard line of his mouth had softened, too. This was the old Shep she knew from Harvard. How she desperately wanted him back! Not the hard, controlling warrior who thought he was in charge of this mission.

"Dad stopped racing sprint cars about ten years ago. Mother pressured him into realizing that as he got older, he needed to start taking better care of himself. She wanted to enter old age with him intact, not in tatters." Maggie chortled at the thought of her mother. "My prim, steel-magnolia Southern mother had a real plan of attack to get my dad away from the sprint car races. I watched her apply that so-subtle pressure on him over a year's time. It was like watching an army general plan strategy and tactics—and win." She smiled fully as she saw Shep's mouth turn up in as wide a smile as he ever gave.

"Southern women have their ways," Shep agreed. He knew Maggie's father was a Northerner, her mother a Southerner from Atlanta. "Does he still have his horse farm in Kentucky?" Because Maggie's father was also a computer manufacturing tycoon, Shep knew the man never wanted for money. He was a billionaire. That status had afforded Maggie the best colleges in the country. But then, she'd earned the right to attend because she was a brilliant woman.

"Yep," Maggie said. She kept most of her attention on the traffic in front and behind them as they moved out of Atlanta, heading in a southeasterly direction toward beautiful Savannah, near the Atlantic Ocean.

"And what about you?" Shep's heart beat a little harder. He really wanted to find out about her life. Had she married and divorced? That information wasn't available in the file he'd read on her. Did she have someone she loved now? Was she in a live-in relationship? In his heart, he didn't want the answer to be yes. Getting to see her again like this was such an unexpected yet wonderfully sweet surprise. Shep found himself jealous of her attention, and confounded by his emotions and reactions. He'd never thought that he could feel now what he had at eighteen years old.

Maggie felt heat stealing up her neck and into her face. Blushing again... With an internal groan, she realized that no matter what her age, she would always be a blusher. Maybe it was because of her red hair; she wasn't sure. Hands tightening momentarily on the wheel, she said flippantly, "Me? I'm up to my rear in bugs at OID. I love my work. I like going into the field and hunting down and identifying an epidemic virus."

"Just like your daredevil father, only you're not racing Thoroughbreds, you're doing something even more dangerous—looking for bacteria and viruses that kill people."

"Are you griping? Or making a statement?"

He chuckled. The sound came from deep within his chest. "You haven't lost your sense of humor, either."

Smiling a little, Maggie moved the automobile into the fast lane and set the cruise control at sixty-five. "My sense of humor has kept me alive, Hunter." She gave him a knowing glance. "Living with you for a year, I had to have a real sense of humor."

Nettled a little by her wry comment, he dropped his brows slightly. Pretending to be checking their route on the onboard computer, he muttered, "It wasn't all thorns and thistles, you know. Or is that all you remember?"

"What do you recall?" Maggie wasn't about to step into *that* trap. No way. She was too frightened of her own feelings, too afraid her clamoring emotions would make her tell Shep how she *really* felt. Maggie didn't want to put herself into that kind of vulnerable position with him. Besides, he'd never give her the same satisfaction. Shep was hard to read. And getting him to talk about how he felt—well, she might as well be a dentist pulling teeth!

Should he tell her? Shep wondered. He wanted to. No, he didn't dare. "I have a tendency to remember the good things we shared, Maggie. Not the bad."

"I don't consider being opinionated bad," she pointed out smartly.

Groaning, he perused the traffic and then used the rearview mirror to once again check the cars around them. "Bullheaded was more like it."

"Are you telling me that in all these years you *still* haven't changed your feelings one iota about women who are smart, savvy and confident? Do you still think we're all stubborn and refuse to bow to your greater intelligence, oh great one?"

"Here we go again!" he growled, giving her a frosty look. "You talk about not changing. Neither have you. In fact, you're worse than I recall."

Maggie's mouth blossomed into a full smile. "Oh, Hunter, you are so archaic. You're worse than that

Neanderthal younger brother of yours, Reid. It's a good thing he married Casey. She'll straighten him out.''

Shep nearly groaned again as he stole a glance at her. She looked delicious. With her dark glasses on, that red-and-gold hair highlighted by the sun behind her, she looked more like a Hollywood starlet than a virologist in that moment. Maggie was not stick thin like those television actresses who looked positively on the brink of starvation. No, she was firm, filled out and supple looking. Although she was short in comparison to him, she had a strong body. Remembering how that body had felt beneath him, he decided to move to a safer subject.

''Tell me, are you still riding hell-bent-for-leather on those eventing horses of yours? Or did you give up the desire to die on one of those jumps, like your dad gave up sprint car racing?''

Laughing delightedly, Maggie wagged a finger at him. ''You're good, Hunter. I'll give you that. This is called let's change topics in midstream so Maggie is thrown off the scent. You never did play fair.''

''And neither did you.''

''You're gloating, Hunter. I can see it even if you don't change the expression on that iceberg face of yours.''

He warmed to her teasing. Their repartee had always been like this. He knew she wasn't being mean or nasty, just teasing him to get him to respond. Granted, he wasn't the most spontaneous person in the world, but life had taught him not to be. In his job, spontaneity could get one killed, and Sarah had died because of just such a spur-of-the-moment decision on his part. Some of the warmth cascading through his chest was doused with sadness over Sarah's untimely death.

"What's wrong?"

Lifting his head, he stared over at Maggie. "What?"

"You're sad."

"I am?" How the hell could she know that? Unsettled, he shifted in the seat.

"Oh, Hunter!" she griped, "You never gave me credit for sensing what you're feeling. Not eighteen years ago. Not *now!* Do you know how *frustrating* that is?" She made a strangled sound in the back of her throat.

"No," he said primly, and began to look around. The traffic was thinning. Along the freeway, roughly a couple of hundred feet on either side of it, grew kudzu, a weed from Japan that had been brought to the States as an ornamental bush and, due to the humid conditions in the South, had spread like a plague. He studied it now, trying to gather his thoughts after her attack.

Maggie gave him a dirty look. Shep seemed impervious to her emotional response. Well, that was just like him. But something was different. Before, he would open up a little bit, show some of his vulnerability to her. Now he had snapped shut, like a proverbial clam. "So, why are you so closed now?" she wondered softly, and sent him a direct glance he couldn't dodge.

Caught. Yep, Maggie had zeroed in on him. Moving uncomfortably and tugging at his flak jacket beneath his shirt, Shep muttered, "Life does it to you, Maggie. You know that."

"Tell me when you started to work for Perseus. I

always thought you loved to fly more than breathe. What took you out of the Air Force and into a merc job?''

Sighing internally, Shep was relieved her questions weren't of a more personal nature. Maggie was too often personal. Feeling edgy, he replied, "I flew Falcons around in the sky until seven years ago. Morgan made a pitch to me that I couldn't resist. I liked the idea of helping people more directly. He used my flying skills for a number of years. I flew one of the Perseus jets for him. I also flew small, single engine planes like the Cessna, too. I was usually involved in missions that required a getaway aircraft on a very short dirt runway. I did a lot of work like that in Africa.''

"Interesting we never ran into one another," Maggie said, "because I've spent almost a third of my professional life over in Africa. Many times, with Casey, on outbreak situations. There, or in South America, in the Amazon region.''

Shep almost said, "I wished we had," but he snapped his mouth shut before the words could blurt out. Traffic was lessening now as they left the sparkling buildings of downtown Atlanta behind them. Ahead of them, he could see both the wide-open grassy flatland and gently rolling hills welcoming them into rural Georgia. Groves of tall, spindly pine trees began to line the freeway like a green wall. Georgia was a pine tree state, there was no doubt, and the lumber industry was going strong, a result of perfect soil and weather conditions for trees to grow fast and tall.

The sky was a bright blue. He could see a few cumulus clouds beginning to form. With the high humidity, cloud formation was inevitable as the sun rose higher in the sky. And then, later in the day, thunderstorms would pop up unexpectedly here and there across the state, but especially along the coast where the mix of warm, humid air created constant instability.

"So…" Maggie said in a low voice, "how has life treated you in the personal department? Did you ever marry? Do you have kids?" She held her breath. Shep hated these kinds of questions and she knew it. But she had nothing to lose and she really did want to know his status. Maggie didn't look too closely at why, however.

Frowning, Shep felt a sharp pain in his chest region. "You haven't lost your touch, have you?"

"What?" she demanded impertinently.

"Oh, come on, Maggie. You always went for the jugular."

"If asking a personal question is the jugular vein for you, Hunter, then something is wrong!"

He saw a pink flush spread across her freckled cheeks, but there was laughter sparkling in her eyes. If anyone but Maggie had asked him those questions, he'd have told them to go to hell in a hurry. "My private life is private. You know that."

"Oh, right. As if mine isn't. You've asked me personal questions and I've answered them, haven't I?"

"Yes."

"Well, it's tit for tat, Hunter. Now you get to answer mine."

"Where's the logic in that?"

She knew he was baiting her. She could sense it. Besides, one corner of his mouth flexed. "Logic dictates that if you ask personal questions of a person, you're basically saying it's okay to have them asked of yourself. It's one of those nonverbal understandings. You know?''

''My questions to you were not *that* personal. Yours are.''

Rolling her eyes in frustration, she nailed him with a dark look. ''Being evasive, are we?''

''My stock and trade, brat.'' Oh, damn! Where had *that* come from? Groaning, Shep held up his hand. ''Sorry, I didn't mean to call you by that name.''

Shaken by the warm intimacy of his endearment for her, Maggie's hands tightened around the steering wheel. Brat had been his intimate name for her, a term used with love. Licking her lips, she carefully felt her way through what he'd just said.

''Are you *really* sorry you used it, Shep?'' Again, she briefly met his gaze. She saw such sadness in his eyes. And longing. For her? For what they'd had, even if it had been rocky, argumentative and imperfect at times? Maggie was unsure of what to make of his slip.

''Well, yes…no… Hell, it just slipped out, Maggie. I'm sorry. That's the past. I guess some things just don't die.''

''They live or die because you want them to.''

It was his turn to feel deeply uncomfortable. Now the car felt claustrophobic. ''Don't make too much out of it, okay? I have a long memory. Some things I just don't forget.''

''Why did you remember my nickname?'' Maggie asked more gently. ''Because you hated me? You're still angry because we broke up instead of getting married? What, Hunter? Is this multiple choice? Do I get to pick?''

"Maggie," he pleaded, holding up his hands, "stop running circles around me. You can outtalk me, I agree. But shooting three or four questions at me isn't going to get any more of a response out of me than one will and you know it."

She grinned a little. "Just like old times, ain't it, Hunter?" And in many ways, she enjoyed their verbal sparring. Sensing the feelings around him, Maggie saw that on one hand, Shep was uncomfortable, but on the other, she was a known entity to him and he knew she would never ever deliberately wound him with her words. That was part of the dance, the cement of their relationship. Their sparring was teasing, but never hurtful.

"Yes," he sighed. "You haven't changed that much, Maggie. You know that?"

Her grin widened. "Thank you. I'll take that as a compliment. As I told you before, neither have you, Hunter."

"So, did you ever get married?"

She stared at him, her mouth opening. She quickly snapped it shut. "What *is* this?" she demanded. "You can ask me highly personal questions, but you don't have to answer mine? Oh, no, Hunter. That's not how this relationship of ours is going, this time. You might have gotten away with these little tactics then, but not now. No way."

"Relationship?"

Groaning, Maggie said, "Wrong word. I didn't mean that. Just because we have to pretend we're married and stay in the same room at night does not a relationship make, okay?"

He grinned. Maggie rarely used the wrong words to describe herself or how she saw the world. The

flush across her cheeks had deepened to a delicious
strawberry color. It made her hazel eyes look like
dancing emeralds set in gold, with a bit of cinnamon
brown in the background. She was so alive to him.
More alive than any other woman he'd ever met. She
was so much like Sarah, and yet Sarah had been a
pale shadow to Maggie's ebullient, sunny personality.
Shep found himself starving for Maggie's quick wit
and the playfulness that she automatically extended
to him. In some ways, Maggie was the same as before. In others, she was better, more polished and
poised. That made him desire her even more.

"For a dyed-in-the-wool wordsmith, Dr. Harper, I
don't think you're in the habit of using wrong words.
So—" he looked at her "—you see what we have
here as a relationship?"

"Hunter, you're not getting one more word out of
me until you answer my questions first. You're not in
control of this situation like you think. I'm your equal
this time around. I'm not some starry-eyed eighteen-
year-old you can intimidate. Does that compute?
Once it does, then I think we can talk and share more.
Yes? No? Tell me how you feel about it."

With a shake of his head, he muttered, "Maggie,
you can run circles around people with that beautiful
mouth of yours. You always could. Maybe you
missed your calling. Instead of a doctor you should
have been a lawyer. Right now, I feel trapped, as if
my arms and legs were tied to steel spikes so I can't
move."

Chuckling and rather pleased with herself, she said
drolly, "Oh, suffer eloquently, Hunter. It's what you
do best, as I recall. You always gave me that puppy-
dog look of hurt in your eyes so I'd ease off. Not this

time. Uh-uh. I'm older and wiser. Nope, the stakes stay in and you're trapped. So you have a choice to make—put up or shut up.''

Checking the traffic one more time, Shep picked up one of the radios and made the obligatory call. Every hour on the hour they were to check in with the FBI and give their location by mile marker, and a status report. He watched Maggie drive as he spoke to the agent at the other end. She was smiling broadly, as if she'd just won a chess game with him. Well, hadn't she? Hanging up the microphone, he slid his arm across the back of her seat. His arm barely touched her proudly thrown back shoulders.

''Because I don't like icy silence for the next hours we have to drive,'' he began in an amused tone, ''I'll answer your questions. No, I'm not married. No, I don't have any children.''

''That's all?''

''What do you mean, 'that's all'? Didn't I answer your questions?''

''Geez Louise, Hunter, you're just so wordy with your answers. You'd think you were in the DA's office being grilled by detectives before your attorney arrived!''

He couldn't help but laugh. ''You know what?'' he said, meeting her gaze, ''I've *really* missed being around you. You're the only one that can pry anything out of me whether I want you to or not.''

Gloating, and warmed by his too rare laughter, Maggie said, ''So, are you in a relationship now?'' A huge part of her hoped not. She saw him hesitate, open his mouth and then close it. He looked away for a long minute before turning his head and meeting her glance once again.

"I was.... But I'm not now." He removed his arm from behind her seat, his hand resting in a closed fist on his thick thigh.

There was pain in his voice, as much as he tried to disguise it, Maggie realized. There was no mistaking the anguish that he tried to hide in his eyes, either. She lost her smile. In that moment, she reached out, her hand covering his. The gesture shocked her as much as it did him. Maggie found his hand felt just as strong as she remembered from decades ago.

"What happened, Shep? I can see it really hurt you."

Glancing at him again, she saw his stony expression and knew he had closed her out once more.

Four

They reached Savannah in the early afternoon. Maggie was glad she knew how stubborn Shep could get because he was closed up so tightly ever since she'd asked about his past that patience was the only answer in dealing with him. He would never give up personal information easily. Maggie knew, as Shep drove them alertly down Interstate 16 towards what she considered the most beautiful city in the South, that Shep was still chewing on the question she'd asked hours earlier.

For just a moment, she allowed her gaze to sweep the antebellum architecture that Savannah was so famous for. From the freeway, she could see the gold dome of city hall. Nearby was the riverfront district, lined with old cotton warehouses now turned into restaurants and gift shops.

The Savannah River, wide and slow moving, had

been a main traffic route in the nineteenth century for ships taking cotton grown in Georgia overseas to English textile mills. Yes, Savannah had a very rich history. The city was semitropical, as it sat seventeen miles from the Atlantic. Hurricanes were the only threat to it. Offshore, as the river opened into the ocean, lay many islands, such as Tybee, Wilmington and Skidaway. The Low Country, as it was referred to, was a busy tourist destination for visitors from around the world.

Off to her left, Maggie could see the world-famous architectural wonder, the Talmadge Memorial Bridge, which spanned the Savannah River and linked Georgia with South Carolina. In her mind, Maggie had always called it Harp Bridge because its structure reminded her of harp strings, strung as it was with thick, strong, white steel cables from a central girder. Sighing softly, she realized she felt at peace, as she always did when she came to Savannah.

Their itinerary called for them to eat at the Olde Pink House Restaurant and Planter's Tavern. A Georgian-style mansion that had been turned into a restaurant, it had a rich and varied history, having been built in the late 1700s for James Habersham, Jr., a wealthy merchant. In the 1800s it had been turned into the Planter's Bank.

As they turned down Abercorn Street, Maggie sighed again. "I can't help it. I think Savannah is the crown jewel of America. Look at the pastel colors of all these beautiful old mansions. It reminds me of driving down the street and looking at prettily colored Easter eggs."

"I like the way you see the world, Maggie," Shep replied casually, though he remained on guard, his gaze sweeping the area as they pulled into a parking lot. Shep knew the reason for this location. It was in the open, not cramped or crowded. He knew FBI agents would be inside and outside, watching them and making sure they were safe. "Easter eggs..." He shook his head, gave her a quick glance and turned off the engine. As he removed his seat belt, he smiled a little. "Only you would see three- to five-story mansions as colored Easter eggs."

The softness of his gaze touched her deeply. Profoundly. Maggie lowered her lashes as she nervously fiddled with her safety belt. "I'm the idealist, Shep. You were always the hard-core realist. All you probably see in these incredibly well-kept mansions is their architecture, not necessarily their outer beauty." She tried to keep her eyes off him. He looked lean, professional in the dark blue sport coat, the white, open-collared shirt and khaki-colored slacks. He was comfortable, but sharp looking, in her opinion. And she knew why he was wearing the sport coat: to hide the weapon he carried. Otherwise, she was sure he'd have shed it long ago in this heat and humidity.

Getting out of the car, he rearranged his sport coat so that the pistol he carried beneath his arm in a holster was hidden from the public as well as the prying eyes of their enemy. Moving around the car, he opened the door for Maggie. She gave him a surprised look.

"I've always been a gentleman," he reminded her archly, holding out his hand to her.

"I'm so used to opening my own doors that I forgot," Maggie said with a sudden laugh. She slid her hand into his. Shep's grip was warm, strong and welcoming. Her fingers were still cool from the nervousness of being around him all these hours.

"Hmm," he said as he pulled her gently upward, "you're not icy feeling anymore."

Without meaning to get so close, Maggie found herself pressed against his tall, powerful frame momentarily. It was shocking. Wonderful. Only their clasped hands remained a barrier between them. But just as quickly, she stepped away. Not before seeing the amusement and longing burn in his eyes as he looked down at her, however. His lips had parted, and suddenly, Maggie knew Shep wanted to kiss her. She stood trapped between the car door and him.

"Easter eggs," Shep murmured as he lowered his head, keeping his hand around hers so she could not escape him. "You know, you're one of a kind, Maggie Harper. Even if you're the most headstrong woman I know, I can't help myself...." And he couldn't. Throughout the drive to Savannah, Shep had been aching to kiss her. To feel Maggie's soft, wide, smiling mouth once more captured by his. Well, they *were* married, weren't they? And if Black Dawn was watching, wouldn't they expect a newly married couple to do things like steal a kiss in a parking lot? Of course. Shep wasn't going to disappoint them. He needed Maggie too much. He'd accepted this assignment because she had been thrown tantalizingly in his path once again. Shep had forever regretted their breakup. Oh, he'd had women and affairs after her, but none of them ever matched Maggie, with her fire and verve.

Maggie's breath caught as she saw the predatory look come to Shep's narrowing eyes. She felt his hand hold hers a little more firmly. Without thinking, she let him gently pull her toward him once again as his head descended toward hers. He was going to kiss her! Stunned, she felt her mind blank out momentarily. It was the last thing she'd expected from him. But then, as she leaned bonelessly against him and felt the hardening of his muscles as he took her weight, her heart burst open with a longing that left her literally breathless in the wake of it.

All the sounds of downtown Savannah—the cars, the horse-drawn buggy clip-clopping nearby—were drowned out beneath the heat in his eyes, the intent clearly written in his face. Yes, this felt right. So very right…Maggie didn't struggle. As she lifted her head to meet his mouth, something old and wonderful broke loose in her wildly beating heart. How much she had missed Shep! Maggie hadn't been aware of it until this precious, unexpected moment. Closing her eyes, she stretched upward as she leaned against him. She felt the moisture of his breath against her cheek. She sensed his nearness. It was a good feeling. So fertile…so desperately needed by her.

When his mouth grazed her parting lips, she quivered. She felt him remove her hand from between them. In moments, her arm was wrapping around his narrow waist as his slid across her shoulders. He brought her gently and fully against him. A sigh rippled from her lips as he grazed them tenderly again. It was that dichotomy about Shep that always threw her. To look at him was to realize this man was a throwback to warriors from the past. In Maggie's heart, she'd always seen him as a crusader from the twelfth century: big, bruising, hard-looking and so very, very powerful. Yet she was privileged to know the other side of him, too, so it was easy to yield to

him completely. With him, she was safe. She knew
he would care for her as if she were a priceless and
fragile treasure.

Moaning, she whispered his name and slid her arm
up across his broad, tense shoulders. Maggie wanted
him. She didn't care who was watching. In this moment, she realized how much she had ached to touch
Shep once again. What they'd shared so long ago was
alive and vivid now. That surprised her, but she
wasn't going to apologize for it, either. As her fingers
slid through the short, sleek hair at the nape of his
neck, she felt his mouth settle powerfully against hers.

His lips moved in a claiming gesture. His breath
was hot against her skin. She opened to him, yielded
to his superior strength because he was tenderly sliding against her, exploring her and reveling in the re-
newal of something that had begun so long ago. Another quiver coursed through her as she felt his arm
move more commandingly down her arched spine, his
large hand settling comfortably against her hips. Yes,
this was the old Shep she knew so well! And she
couldn't get enough of him and that teasing, heated
mouth of his. The roughness of his beard caused a
delicious, prickling sensation against her skin. The
male odor of him entered her flaring nostrils as she
responded strongly to his pressure upon her mouth.
Fingers sliding provocatively through his hair, she felt
him shudder. As she drowned in the sunlit offering
of his mouth, she felt him opening to her on all levels.
Maggie felt the controlled power of him as he rav-
ished her lips. This was heaven. *He* was her heaven.
Oh, why had they broken up so long ago? It seemed
so silly now.

Maggie didn't want the exploratory kiss to

end…and she moaned a little in frustration as his mouth lifted reluctantly from her wet, slick lips. Slowly looking up, she drowned in the dark, stormy color of his eyes as he studied her in the intense moments after their kiss. Her mouth curved recklessly. "You've gotten better with age, Shep."

His returning smile was filled with mirth. "Why did I ever leave you, Maggie?" And with a shake of his head, he eased her from the safety of his embrace. She was soft and curvy in all the right places. He liked a woman with some meat on her bones. Stick women never turned him on. Maggie was well built, firm and in tremendous athletic condition. It made him burn with desire for her, with the urge to consummate what he knew was theirs to take with one another.

"I don't know…." She said softly, captured in his burning gaze, which scorched her like a delicious, sweeping fire. But she did know. The passion had always been strong between them. That hadn't changed. But she also knew there were things about this man that drove her crazy. How he hadn't always trusted her abilities. Or seen her as an equal. And yet, she'd seen the respect in his gaze for her today during his unguarded moments and that made her feel good about herself.

Running her fingers up the sleeve of his jacket, she whispered, "Maybe being eighteen-year-olds with no maturity or experience behind us made us act a little too rashly?" She was still thunderstruck by the power of his kiss—and the feelings in her it had aroused.

Capturing her hand, Shep forced himself to step back. The late sun beat down on them, and sweat trickled down his rib cage. He hungered for Maggie, who had the sweetest look on her upraised face. In her hazel eyes, he saw desire for him alone. It made him feel strong and good about himself. "Maybe so, brat...." He hesitated, then took another step back, with a slight smile of apology. "Damn, I can't seem to kick the habit of calling you by my favorite nickname. Sorry." And he was. Moving to the rear of the car, he opened the trunk and lifted out the aluminum suitcase containing the fake anthrax. He handed it to Maggie, because she was the official courier.

"Why?" Maggie moved aside and allowed him to shut and lock the door. "I *liked* my nickname. I earned it, remember?" She felt the weight of the suitcase in her left hand and remembered why they were together. And the danger they were in. It washed away some of her euphoria. If Black Dawn were here, she and Shep could be taken out in two shots. Both of them could be dead. Suddenly, she rebelled at the danger. She'd just found Shep again! Why couldn't they have met some other way? Somewhere safer? Less intense? All at once every touch of his hand on hers she absorbed fully, feeling the importance of every second, every minute spent with him.

Chuckling, Shep held her hand as they walked toward the front door of the restaurant. "So, if I slip again, you're not going to throw a book at me or something?" On guard once again, he was checking out pedestrians on either side of the street, which was clogged with traffic and cars at this time of day. He was looking for anything unusual or out of place. Shep knew that from rooftops around this restaurant, FBI agents in battle gear, with sniper's rifles, were discreetly watching them through their scopes.

"Of course not," Maggie said with a laugh.

"Granted, I was a hothead back then, but I've mellowed a little since."

"Really? You could have fooled me." He grinned sheepishly and added in a confidential tone, "That's good to know." He opened the door for her and allowed her entrance into the restaurant. He smiled a little as he remembered how, when they were younger, Maggie had more than once sent a book sailing across the room at him when she got really angry. Of course, Shep acknowledged as they were led up to the second floor of the restaurant, he'd probably had it coming, because he would mercilessly provoke her sometimes just to see that redheaded anger of hers explode. Making up was always such a delicious reward, and that's why he usually did it. Shep gazed around the remarkable, historic restaurant. There were oil paintings of the residents of old Savannah. Even one of George Washington, and of course, the owner of the mansion, Habersham, in gaudy-looking shoe and knee buckles.

As Maggie sat down and accepted a menu, she glowed. "This is the best window in the place, Shep." After giving their drink orders of iced tea, they were left alone. "Look," Maggie said excitedly as she pointed out the window. "There's Reynolds Square. Isn't it beautiful?"

"What I'm looking at is beautiful," Shep murmured as he closed his menu. Maggie flushed. Beautifully. He ached to reach over and undo that chignon at the base of her long, lovely neck. Though he told himself that it was bad timing, he enjoyed seeing how his flattery made her glow even more.

"Shep…"

"Well, it's the truth, Maggie." He glanced out the

window. The tree-covered square was one of many in the heart of downtown Savannah. Each square was unique and beautiful in its own right. Around each were the antebellum mansions—the Easter eggs, as Maggie referred to them—that brought such rainbow colors to this incredible city. "I think the maître d' brought us to the most romantic table in the restaurant."

"He did," she said. Maggie looked around. At this hour, after the lunch-hour crowd, there were not many diners, which was good as far as she was concerned. It meant less people to keep tabs on while they ate. "This is one of my favorite places to dine. It's so rich in history."

"And you always loved history."

"Yes," she said softly. "I still love it."

"We have a lot of ancient history between us, you know. Dinosaurs, maybe?"

She chuckled. "So, we're two ancient people."

"I'd never say you looked like a dinosaur, Maggie. You look beautiful and fresh to me. History helps us understand the past. What we did right…or wrong. The good or bad decisions we made."

She arched inwardly at his gruffly spoken words, allowing his compliments to touch her opening heart, wanting desperately for him to kiss her once again. She struggled to maintain some decorum in the restaurant. He looked sad after he spoke the words. But she didn't get a chance to ask him about them, as the waitress brought iced tea with fresh sprigs of mint in it and bright yellow crescents of lemon on a doily-covered plate. Maggie sighed. "I'm going to enjoy my meal, Hunter." She looked up at the waitress and said, "I've *got* to have your wonderful she-crab soup laced with sherry, and that to-die-for Caesar salad with cornbread oysters as my main course.''

Shep absorbed Maggie's gusto for living. Everything she did she did with passion, with excitement and intensity. Her eyes were sparkling like jewels as she gave the order to the blond waitress attired in a white cotton blouse and black slacks.

''And you, sir?'' the waitress inquired.

Shep looked at Maggie. ''You know this place. What would I like to eat?''

Thrilled, because they had done this long ago with one another, Maggie laughed and looked up at the waitress. ''This guy will eat half a steer in one sitting if you don't watch him. Give him a 'welcome to the South' meal of sautéed shrimp with country ham and grits. He'll take the she-crab soup, too, and a small dinner salad with blue cheese dressing on the side.''

Shep leaned back, feeling pleased. Maggie hadn't forgotten one thing about him...even his favorite salad dressing. Amazed and still a little dazed over their kiss, their rekindling of what he'd thought had died long ago, he felt a new determination sweep through him. He'd lost Sarah. He wasn't about to lose Maggie. No...he just couldn't. Remembering that terrible day doused much of Shep's current happiness. If only he'd kept a better eye on Sarah. If only he hadn't let the situation get out of hand, Sarah might be alive today. Well, that wasn't going to happen now. Maggie was here and she was alive. And his heart shrank in terror at the thought of having a terrorist's bullet rip through her vital, beautiful body and steal her away from him.

As he gazed around the room out of habit, he wondered why he was being given a second chance with

Maggie. Her kiss had been wonderfully revealing—soft, feminine, strong and sweet. Wherever she had touched his body with her own, he could still feel the tingles, the yearning.

"Why are you looking so sad?" Maggie asked as she sipped her iced tea.

Startled, he stared at her momentarily. And then he remembered just how well Maggie could read him, no matter how he tried to maintain a poker-faced expression. "Can't hide much from you, can I?" He played with the silverware absently. "Yeah," he finally responded, "I'm a little sad."

Tilting her head, Maggie asked, "Why?" She saw grief in his eyes, combined with a hard determination.

"After we broke up," he began in a low tone, "I swore off women for a long time." He moved the fork around in his fingers and stared down at it for some moments. "And then, gradually, over time, I got back into socializing more. I never met anyone like you, so I never got married…until…later, when things changed." His brows drew together. "When I went to work with Perseus, Morgan teamed me up with a partner. That was his mandate—everyone had to have a partner. Well, I rebelled on that one, but if I wanted to work for him, I had to go along with company policy. So I did." He lifted his gaze to hers. "My partner was a woman named Sarah Collier. She was an ex-marine sniper and damn good at what she did. We were partners for three years, until I did something very stupid that I'll pay for forever."

Maggie placed her elbows on the table and cradled her chin on her clasped hands. Raw anguish burned in Shep's eyes. She felt a terrible sense of grief and guilt surround him as he restlessly rolled the fork back and forth across the white linen tablecloth in front of him. "What happened, Shep?"

"I got her killed in the line of duty," he answered flatly. He stopped rolling the fork around. Forcing himself, he looked across the table at Maggie. "We were in Macedonia on an undercover assignment to find this little girl who had been kidnapped by the Serbs. There were thousands of mines all over that area. Maybe a million. I don't know." He shrugged his shoulders painfully in remembrance. "We'd found the girl. She was alive. Unharmed, thank God. We were being pursued by her captors and we came upon this open farm field. Sarah said we should go around it. She warned me about the mines. I made a command decision to cross it. I had the six-year-old in my arms and we started running because we could hear the enemy in hot pursuit. All we had to do was make it across that field, to the trees, and we'd be safe." His mouth hardened and he looked away, the memory fresh and hurting.

"In my hurry to cut off a minute of time because I didn't feel we had it, I risked all our lives. I knew there were mines all over the damned place. I knew it...." He gripped the fork so hard that his fingers whitened around the utensil. "Sarah was leading the way. I was running and bringing up the rear. She was two hundred feet ahead of me, being the point person, paving the way for us. She was the one taking the risks...."

Maggie closed her eyes when she saw tears gleam momentarily in Shep's slitted gaze, his mouth forced into a suffering line. "Oh, no.... Don't tell me she stepped on a mine?"

He nodded, the words choked in his throat. The

look on Maggie's face made him want to cry. How easily touched she was! How wonderfully sensitive she was to the human condition…and to him. "Don't feel sorry for me in this," he growled. "I was the stupid bastard who was in a hurry, remember? If I hadn't been so damned much in a hurry that morning, she'd be alive today…."

"And were you or the child hurt?"

"No…"

Gently, Maggie said, "Shep, I think Sarah knew what she was doing. She understood the risks. And who is to say that the minute you cut off by going through the field instead of around it *didn't* save your lives? Can you be really sure that your decision wasn't sound, under the circumstances?"

Painfully, he lifted his shoulders. "It was more than that, Maggie. Over the years, I had fallen in love with Sarah. I finally figured what life was about. I had finally found a woman somewhat like you…." He gazed at Maggie fiercely. "But she wasn't you. She had some of your attributes…."

"I'm sure you loved her for all the right reasons," Maggie whispered. Without thinking, she reached over and captured Shep's left hand. "I'm so sorry, Shep. For both of you. Sarah sounded like a very, very brave, competent woman."

Gripping Maggie's warm fingers, he gave her a measured look. "I'll tell you one thing, brat, I'm *never* going to allow that to happen again. After Sarah died, I came off that mission and told Morgan that I was either going solo on missions from that time onward or he could fire me. At that time, I didn't care, I was so full of grief and guilt. As it was, I hit the bottle. I drank the pain away. It took me more than a year to pull myself out of it, and to be honest, if Morgan hadn't been there to kick my butt all over the place, I'd probably still be in a dark bar somewhere drinking away my guilt.''

Her heart twinged with grief. Maggie saw that the guilt was still there. ''Listen to me, Shep—you saved that little girl's life. Two people walked away from something that might have killed all of you. Have you looked at it from that angle?''

He release her fingers reluctantly. ''Sure I have. But SOP—standard operating procedure—said to avoid open fields. They were well known to have mines planted throughout them. I disobeyed. I was arrogant. I thought I knew what was best for all of us....''

Tenderly, she moved her fingers across his outstretched hand. ''You are a little arrogant. But many times, you know a lot, Shep. That doesn't mean you don't listen to good people who know things, too.''

''As you pointed out long ago,'' he muttered, ''that was one of my failings, one of the things that broke us up.''

Chuckling slightly, Maggie said, ''How well I remember. You had all the good ideas and I had none.'' And now she saw how that attitude had gotten him tangled up in the mission with Sarah. Maggie would never know what the right answer had been on that mission. She hadn't been there and there was no way to judge if Shep had really made a wrong decision or not. But he believed he had. Obviously.

''On this mission,'' he warned her gravely, ''I'm not going to lose you. I swore I'd never take on a partner again and Morgan knew that. But when he showed me your photo, told me that you were volunteering to set yourself up as a decoy to try and capture Black Dawn terrorists, my heart got ahead of my head and my past experiences didn't matter. I told Morgan I wanted it. I wanted you as my partner. He about fell off his chair. I think he thought he was going to have to argue long and hard for me to take this mission with you—but he was wrong. You're too beautiful, Maggie, too alive. You deserve the best protection in the world on this top event. If I'd known ahead of time, I'd have talked you out of it. This mission is lethal. You could be killed.''

Shep shifted uncomfortably in the chair. ''I came because I want you to walk out of this mission alive and in one piece. I've learned a lot since Sarah's death. I'll control this situation completely this time. I'll make sure you survive it.''

Uneasily, Maggie studied him, heard the steel resolve in his deep baritone voice. ''Shep,'' she begged gently, ''don't say you're going to control this situation. That's what probably got you into that position with Sarah. If you *had* listened to her, things might have turned out differently. Don't you see? You *were* controlling her and the decisions at that time. Frankly, I would hope that you'd listen to my input. Granted, I'm not up on stealth tactics, but I've got two eyes, good intuition and a fair amount of practicality. I'd hope you'd listen to me. We're a team on this, Shep.''

Shaking his head, Shep growled, ''This isn't up for discussion, Maggie. I'm keeping you safe on this mission. There's no way I'm putting you in jeopardy like I did Sarah. I lost one woman I loved. I'm not about to do it twice. No way in hell.''

She opened her mouth and then closed it. What was Shep really saying? That he couldn't trust her? That she was a mute partner in this deadly dance they were on? That her input didn't matter? Bristling internally, Maggie capped her emotional reaction. Right now, Shep was raw with guilt over Sarah's death. He'd loved her. Well, Maggie was sure his reaction didn't mean he loved *her*. Maggie and Shep had a past history with one another and with his overprotective nature, she was sure he couldn't help taking charge on this mission.

Out of the corner of her eye, Maggie saw the waitress approaching with their soup. "I'm tabling this discussion for now," she warned him in a low voice, "but once we get to our bed and breakfast later, we need to talk more. Okay?"

The resolve in Maggie's tone shook him. This wasn't a soft, willowy eighteen-year-old talking to him. No, it was a mature, confident woman. It brought back vivid memories of Sarah's confidence. She had been rock solid as a warrior and could always be relied upon to give her best. She'd never let Shep down in the three years they were paired. Not once. It was *he* who had let *her* down. Well, Maggie thought she could be like Sarah, but she couldn't. Not on this mission. No, Maggie needed his protection and experience. Whether she agreed with him or not, Shep was going to fully control their situation. Every minute of it. Somehow, if he could complete this mission successfully, he knew that he could assuage some of his guilt where Sarah was concerned. If he could get Maggie safely through this gauntlet, maybe some of this terrible guilt would stop eating him alive and life would look a little more hopeful to him than it did now. That was all he asked for.

Five

Just as they were leaving the restaurant, Shep's cell phone, which he carried in his sport coat jacket, beeped. Reaching out, he pulled Maggie aside in the lobby. Automatically, he placed himself in front of her and the doors of the restaurant—just in case.

"Yes?" he growled into the phone.

Maggie felt tension sizzling from Shep. His eyes narrowed and became icy with only a bare hint of blue in their depths. Understanding that the FBI had just phoned, she figured the call was more than likely a warning. Maggie's focus shifted from her personal thoughts to the dangers that surrounded them. Gripping the attaché case in her left hand, she kept her right hand free in case she had to pull out the pistol she carried in her purse. Though the traffic outside looked normal, Maggie knew the terrorists' best cover was their ability to fade into the fabric of the world around them. A professional terrorist never stood out like the proverbial sore thumb, she thought grimly as she watched Shep click off the cell phone and jam it back into his pocket.

"Trouble?" she guessed.

"Yes. They've spotted a black luxury sedan that has gone around this block four times in a row. Two men are in it. The feds are running the plates right now. A sniper on the building across the street noticed them." Shep glanced down at her. "We're staying put until we know more."

Maggie felt his tremendously protective nature now; it flowed around her powerfully. The fact that Shep had automatically positioned his bulk in front of her, in case bullets came flying through the glass of the doors toward them, wasn't lost on her. He stood slightly slouched, his feet apart like a boxer waiting to receive a blow. She was getting a taste of the warrior in Shep. Right now, her heart was beating hard in her breast and she was scared. Gulping, her throat dry with the adrenaline coursing through her, she whispered, "Do terrorists always drive such fancy cars?"

"Not necessarily," he said, his gaze fastened on the slowly moving traffic on the street in front of them. It was rush hour now, five o'clock, and the traffic had increased substantially. "They usually don't use high end, expensive cars because they stand out too much. This is probably nothing to worry about, but I'm not in the business of taking chances." Especially with Maggie at his side.

Somehow, Shep told himself, he was going to have to get her through this in one piece. At the other end of this mission, he wanted—no, demanded—time alone with her. More than anything, he realized suddenly, he wanted to reestablish a personal connection with Maggie. His lips tingled hotly in memory of her soft, yielding kiss against his mouth. She'd kissed him back. She'd wanted to kiss him as eagerly as he had. After all these years, a spark had exploded between them like a candle lighting the darkness of his wounded heart. For him, Maggie symbolized a freedom he'd found only with her. Now, as he stood with his knees slightly bent, prepared for an attack, he wanted that brass ring. He wanted Maggie. All of her. To hell with consequences.

The cell phone rang again. Shep pulled it from his pocket and flipped it open. His features were grim as he said, "Yes?"

Maggie gazed tensely out the restaurant doors. This was downtown Savannah, and at rush hour it was always better to walk in the beautiful squares rather than drive. Her gaze moved from one building top across the street to the next. She couldn't see any of the FBI snipers who were hidden up there for their protection. They were doing a good job of staying out of sight.

"I see… Thanks…"

Maggie turned her attention to Shep. He put the cell phone away. "Trouble?"

"No. A false alarm."

"Probably tourists looking for a parking spot to come here and eat at rush hour. Bad combination," Maggie said with a slight smile. "This time of day, you can circle a square for half an hour before you find a parking spot."

Shep nodded. He moved forward and opened the

door for her. "Let's go. And let's stay on alert. I don't have a good feeling about this."

As they walked down the street, Shep moved to the curb side, his arm going around Maggie's waist. He drew her close in a protective gesture. The sunlight was hot and intense, the humidity still high. Above the buildings Maggie could see cumulus clouds thickening into mighty thunderheads. She wouldn't be surprised if it stormed tonight, judging from the size of them.

Shep's long stride was making her take two steps for his every one. He suddenly sensed she was having to almost skip to keep up with him, and he instantly slowed his pace. Liking the curve of his hand around her waist, Maggie smiled to herself. How wonderful it had been to simply talk to Shep. For once he was forthcoming and not as closed up as usual. Or maybe life had made him more accessible than he had been in his younger years? Maggie fervently hoped so.

"I'll drive," Shep said, opening the door.

"No, it's my turn."

"Maggie—"

"Hey, it's my turn, remember?"

Tensely, Shep gazed around the parking lot which was now filled with people arriving to eat at the famous restaurant. Every one of them was a potential terrorist threat as far as he was concerned. Losing patience as Maggie moved to sit in the driver's seat, Shep gripped her arm and stopped her.

"Not now, Maggie. We'll fight some other time."

Jerking her arm out of his grasp, she glared up at him. "Use your head, Hunter. I *know* this city. You don't. If we get attacked, who is going to know the ins and outs, the back alleys and the best ways to avoid the attack? It sure won't be you.''

Frowning, he watched as she disregarded his orders and sank belligerently into the driver's seat. He almost reached out and pulled her out. *No.* Now was not the time to get into one of their squabbles. This was just like before, when they were living with one another. Didn't she realize that he should have control because he knew best in this situation? Frustrated, he stalked angrily around the car, jerked open the passenger door and got in.

Maggie started the car after closing her door. She felt anger radiating from Shep. She saw it in the hard, unhappy line of his mouth. ''I know where the Crescent Bed and Breakfast is located.''

''I've changed my mind,'' he told her gruffly, and pulled out his cell phone. ''We're not going there. I have a bad feeling and I don't like it.''

Maggie stared at him. ''But...the FBI are there. We'll be safe....''

''The FBI don't guarantee a damn thing, Maggie.'' He got his contact, Agent Caldwell, on the phone. ''Yeah, we're going to avoid the bed and breakfast. I want to change our plans. We'll head up toward Hilton Head Island and pick a random place to stay. It's only an hour from here. If we're getting tailed, this will throw them off. If we act like we're easy targets, they might get suspicious and think it's a trap. We've got to make them think otherwise. If we seem likely to escape, Black Dawn will get bold and strike.''

Rolling her eyes, Maggie sat back and waited until he was off the phone. ''Just because you don't get to drive, you're going to blow a place that's protected by our side?''

"That's not the reason," he said as he looked around. "Let's go. You know how to get to Hilton Head via the freeway?"

"Of course I do." With a shake of her head, Maggie backed the car out of the slot. Once on the street, she made the necessary turns to head back onto the interstate. It was five-thirty, with plenty of daylight left. The drive to Hilton Head was on a four-lane freeway, through rolling countryside. It was a relatively untraveled route, so they could easily spot a tail.

Once on the freeway, they found the traffic still congested for the first couple of miles, with commuters heading home for the evening. The sky ahead was dotted with thunderstorms that were building up and looming menacingly. Maggie wondered if they'd get the storms as they moved in a northeasterly direction toward Hilton Head. Since it was off the coast of South Carolina, and there was so much ocean humidity and warmth, she knew the chance for storms increased proportionately.

Shep continued to gaze around and keep track of the cars nearby. His tightened gut eased only a little. Something was wrong; he could feel it. He couldn't say *what* it was; he only knew he felt stalked by the terrorists. His gut feeling had saved his life too many times before for him to question his decision now. He glanced over at Maggie's set profile. He knew she thought he was being controlling again—a know-it-all. Well, he wasn't.

"I really think this is a mistake, Shep. You blow a perfectly good place that's protected and throw us out in the unknown." Maggie pointed to the clouds ahead. "And on top of that, we're going to get nailed

tonight with a lot of thunderstorms up in the Hilton
Head area. That's not good. You can't hear anything
coming with the thunder bouncing around. Rain could
play a dangerous part if we can't hear terrorists approaching.''

''Your protest is noted,'' he said heavily. ''You can
put it in your after-action report when we get through
this mess in one piece.''

''I don't like your sarcasm. You're belittling me—
again. Just like you did when we were together.'' Her
fingers tightened around the steering wheel. ''Damn,
some things just don't change. I was hoping you'd be
more reasonable.''

''Maggie…don't start.…''

Glaring at him for a moment, she returned her attention to the traffic. ''You didn't even bother to consult me, Shep. That's what I don't like. You couldn't
care less what I think, and that really makes me angry.
Well, I'm not some airhead eighteen-year-old, all
right? I'm thirty-six and I damn well have some experience of the world. You should be taking advantage of my knowledge, not canning it like it doesn't
count.''

Her nostrils flared and she tried to shake the anger
she felt toward him, but to no avail. ''A leopard never
changes his spots. That's *you,* Hunter.''

Holding up his hand, he watched the traffic thinning dramatically now. Ahead of them the freeway
was nearly empty as they drove toward Hilton Head.
''Look, I made a military strategy decision. You've
got to *trust* me during times like this. I had a gut
feeling on this, Maggie.'' He drilled her with a dark
look. ''I suppose you're going to tell me that

women's intuition counts for something, but if a man has intuition, it doesn't work the same way?''

"You're so good at holding ground and arguing your points as to why your decision is the best one, Hunter.'' Maggie met his gaze sadly. "I'm disappointed in you, that's all. And if you think for a moment you're going to keep this up without my input, you are dead wrong.''

Wearily, he said, "Let's use our energy, our alertness for the enemy. Let's not be taking pounds of flesh out of each other, okay? We agree to disagree. Let's leave it at that.''

How could she enjoy kissing him so much one moment, and then have him backhand her like this when it came to such an important decision? Maggie knew she wasn't being overly dramatic. Shep's call could mean life or death. Her reaction wasn't irrational at all. But he didn't get that. He never did. "Some things never change,'' she told him bitterly. "Fine, I'll shut up. But if I see something or feel something about this mission, I'm going to be in your face, Hunter. And next time, I'm not going to be sweet or yielding about it. You got that?''

Now he was tasting Maggie the warrior. He could tell the way her hazel eyes blazed with controlled anger that she damn well meant every word. "Fine,'' he muttered. "I'll try to listen to you.''

Well, that wasn't going to happen. Shep knew best. His thoughts moved ahead. Calling up the computer maps of the area, he studied them in tense silence. Soon the light changed. Looking up, he saw ragged gray-and-white cauliflower-shaped clouds blotting out the sun. He hoped it wouldn't rain. Rain and thunder, as Maggie had rightly pointed out, could benefit the terrorists, allowing them to approach without detection. It was a dangerous situation.

Shrugging off his apprehension, Shep took a deep breath. He felt better being on the road again. Moving targets were harder to take out than sitting ducks in a bed and breakfast. So the FBI had to scramble now, trying to tail them and get ahead of them. That was part of their job. Shep was in charge. He made the final calls on this mission. If the FBI team was upset, then so were the terrorists. And that was just what Shep had intended. Black Dawn would never suspect a trap—they'd be too busy trying to keep up.

Fuming, Maggie kept her attention on her driving. Taking Route 278, they made a wide, looping turn over two arching bridges that spanned salt marshes, taking them to the posh Hilton Head Island, where the rich and famous lived. The island was shaped like a human foot, quite literally. Maggie had friends who lived on the island retreat. It was surrounded by dark green tidal wetlands, home to many different types of shorebirds and waterfowl, including the magnificent great blue heron, whose wingspan was seven feet wide.

"Do you have *any* idea where you want to stay?" she demanded icily. Above them, the skies were turning turbid and threatening. Soon, the first approaching thunderhead would hit the island with well-known summer fury and power. The unstable, humid air of the coast bred some of the most violent thunderstorms Maggie had ever seen. The traffic was thickening again. It was 6:20 p.m.—time for tourists to be leaving the island and residents to be trying to get home. Traffic on Hilton Head was terrible, in her opinion,

confined to two-way streets for the most part, except
for two main arteries that were blessedly four lane.

"I have several options, according to the computer
list."

"Well, why don't you ask me? I've lived in this
area. I know this island like the back of my hand.
See, Shep? Even now you'd rather rely on a damned
computer than ask me what I know."

Rankled, he glanced over at her with apology in
his eyes. "Okay, you're right. So what do you sug-
gest?"

Frustration ate at Maggie. "I think we should stick
close to 278, the only main route off this island if
things go bad and we need to run. I think we should
go to the Hilton Head Plantation area. There are a lot
of time-share resorts down there and there's bound to
be a last-minute cancellation at one of those villas.
It's summer, so it's peak season here." She gripped
the wheel nervously. "We'll just have to take our
chances. It might mean stopping at a few time-share
offices."

He shrugged. "Sounds good to me." Shep knew
the FBI could locate them at all times. There was a
device in the car that constantly transmitted their position to a satellite, and then to their mobile computer
base. He knew there were four technicians in the
white van, plus a driver and guard. It was, quite literally, headquarters for this operation. From the van,
which he knew was probably ten miles behind them,
any and all law enforcement could be called in to
assist them at a moment's notice. The thought was
comforting.

"I'm going to try and situate us at Skull Creek
Marina, on the north side of the island. If things get

dicey, we can always jump into a boat and escape. I don't think Black Dawn will have a boat around here, do you?''

"It's a good idea, having a second type of transportation to rely on," he agreed. He saw Maggie arch beneath his compliment. She was right: he really needed to bring her into the loop on this mission a lot more than he had. As usual, he was thinking that his partner didn't know the area—but she did. Shep pointedly reminded himself to take advantage of her expertise.

Maggie turned off onto Whooping Crane Way. The traffic was stop and go. She felt better with Shep taking her advice. Finally, after fifteen minutes, they reached the Skull Creek Marina. It was on a deep, quiet inlet guarded by several small islands. The marshy islands reminded Maggie of a series of stones set in a necklace. A much larger island beyond— Pickney Island Wildlife Refuge—afforded thousands of migrating birds a roost at different times of the year.

Maggie saw the marina ahead. Everything from million-dollar yachts, to bass boats, and even a few aluminum fishing boats with outboard motors on back, made this harbor their home. With the threat of thunderstorms, the smooth, mirrorlike water looked like black marble.

"There's a nice time-share known as the Great Blue Heron Resort just down this street."

"Let's try for it."

Pleased, Maggie made a right turn. ''This particular time-share is right on the water, and the marina is steps away from it. I'm trying to strategically situate us so we have more escape options, if it comes to that.''

"Good thinking," he exclaimed. Why in hell didn't he consult more with her? Maggie had her head on straight.

He knew why. Sarah. The mistake he'd made with her. Rubbing his jaw in discomfort, Shep watched as the tightly packed houses, each worth millions, he was sure, opened up to a three-story, blue-gray building that had a sign with a great blue heron carved on it. Maggie turned in.

"Nice looking."

"It is." She pointed to the marina, which was truly within walking distance. "Hope it has a cancellation."

"We'll find out soon enough," Shep said.

"I think this is Maggie Harper luck," Shep said as they drove back to the isolated time-share. They'd been fortunate; a family of six had canceled and a second-floor villa was open for the taking. Shep typed in their location on the laptop computer, gave their room number and sent off the e-mail message. The mobile HQ would pick it up. The FBI would then, within the next hour, establish a new perimeter of defense to wait and watch.

Pleased, Maggie smiled as she parked the car in the garage below the villas. "It's nice to be here. I like being near the ocean." As she opened the door, the first carom of thunder rolled across the area. It sounded like someone was pounding a huge kettle-drum above their heads. She and Shep quickly removed their luggage from the trunk and headed to the stairs at the side of the building. Palm trees, cypress,

pecan and live oak surrounded the place. High hedges
also promised privacy. Hurrying up the stairs, Maggie
was relieved to get to their villa.

Once inside unit 214, Maggie saw two bedrooms
off to the left and one down at the end of a long hall
on her right. The decor was cheery, the bamboo furniture covered with cushions in bright, tropical prints.
The kitchen was painted a warm yellow, and there
was a bar where people could eat, as well as a formal
dining room that had a large bamboo-and-glass table.

"Nice place," she murmured, and started down the
hall to the right.

"Hold it," Shep cautioned. He held up his hand,
locked the door behind them. Motioning to the left,
he said, "Let's stay together. You take one of these
two bedrooms. If something happens, we don't want
to be separated, okay?"

Hesitating, Maggie stood in the living room, her
luggage in hand. "Okay…" She turned and walked
down the teak-floored hall which gleamed golden-
brown beneath the lights. The bedrooms were for
children, with two twin beds in each one. Maggie
chose the dark green bedroom and wearily put her
luggage on a bed. This room, too, had a tropical motif
and thick, cushiony bamboo chairs.

Poking her head out, she said, "I'm going to take
a quiet, hot shower, Hunter. Don't disturb me unless
they come smashing through the front door, okay?"

He ambled down the hall and stood just outside her
door. Each room had its own private bathroom. Maggie looked drawn and tired. He could see slight shadows beneath her beautiful green-and-gold eyes.
"Yeah, go ahead. I'll play watchdog. When you get
done, it's my turn."

Maggie entertained the thought of sharing a shower with Shep. It had been one of their favorite activities after making love. And many times it resulted in making love all over again beneath those wonderful streams of warm water. She saw a gleam in his eyes and sensed he was thinking the exact same thing. Heat rose in her neck and flowed into her face. Damn, she was blushing. Turning away, but not before she saw the corners of his mouth lift a little, she muttered. "Why don't you call for pizza delivery or something? We had a late lunch, but there's no food in this place. I don't want to go to another restaurant. I'd just like to sit and rest."

Nodding, he said, "It's a good idea. But let's discuss it later?"

The shower was her way of unwinding from her dangerous job at the OID.

Maggie quickly rubbed a dark green cloth with some jasmine-scented soap. Outside she could hear thunder rumbling again and again. The stained-glass window above her, which depicted a great blue heron standing elegantly in a marsh, was splattered with rain pouring from the sky.

Shep was sitting on the bamboo couch, several maps spread out on the glass table in front of him, when Maggie emerged. She had changed into a pair of comfortable jeans, dark brown loafers and a short-sleeved pink blouse with shell buttons and some lace around the Peter Pan collar. Running her fingers nervously through her damp hair, she absorbed the powerful intent in his eyes as he looked up. Maggie felt his desire for her. It was a wonderful discovery. She reveled in the sensation. Her body tightened and she ached once more to kiss him. The situation didn't merit such a possibility. Right now, Maggie understood how volatile a game they were playing. Lightning flashed nearby and she watched the sky light up outside the double glass doors that led to a spacious screened-in porch.

"Looks like we're in for it," she murmured, moving to the bar and sitting on one of the stools.

In more ways than one, Shep thought. How provocative Maggie looked, her face flushed from the heat of her bath and her hair mussed from the humidity. Even without makeup, she looked incredibly beautiful. Maggie had a charisma that drew him powerfully to her. The soft, flexible way her lips moved entranced him. How desperately he wanted to taste the honey, the sweetness of her once more.

"I'm going to go get that pizza you suggested," he said. "I'll fetch it now, while it's still light. I don't want anyone coming to the door, Maggie. Your idea about getting some food for later is good." He jabbed a finger at the local map of the island. "I see there's a pizza parlor at the marina. It's close and handy. Now that you're out of the shower, I'll go pick one up." He lifted his head. "You still like anchovies on your pizza?"

She grinned. "Always. Half with anchovy, half with pepperoni, right?" Her eyes gleamed with laughter, with tenderness.

It was like old times to Shep. He disliked anchovies. Maggie loved them with a passion. Their tastes were just like everything else in their relationship—opposite. Rising, he shrugged on his sport coat to hide his weapon. "You don't forget a thing," he told her in amazement. Moving toward the door, he said, "I'll knock three times and give you the code for the day.

Then you let me in. Otherwise, don't answer this door—or the phone—for any reason while I'm gone.'' He drilled her with a dark look. The set of her lips told him she didn't like being told what to do. "Please?"

Softening a little, Maggie said, "Okay, I won't answer the door."

"This should take about twenty or twenty-five minutes," he said as he opened the door and checked the hallway.

"You're going to get rained on, Hunter."

He grinned slightly. "Yeah, well, just deserts for my bullheadedness, right?"

Laughing, Maggie slid off the bar stool and sauntered to the foyer, where he stood with the door open. It was pouring outside. "We could be at the bed and breakfast in Savannah enjoying a nice, comfy evening, you know."

"This is a better way to go," he assured her confidently. As he moved out into the hall, Shep decided not to tell Maggie that the FBI had been delayed by an accident on the highway leading into Hilton Head. He didn't want her worried or upset that they were without protection right now. What she didn't know wouldn't hurt her. Besides, as long as she followed orders and kept the door locked, she'd be fine for the twenty minutes he'd be gone. "I'll see you in a little bit," he promised, and left.

Maggie made sure the door was locked in his absence. Turning around, she decided to watch television. At least she could catch the national news. Sitting down after adjusting the television, she sighed and pushed off her shoes. Wriggling her toes in the thin, white cotton socks, she stretched out on the couch. Closing her eyes, she promised herself she wouldn't fall asleep. But she did within moments. The stress and danger of the day had taken its toll.

The banging at the front door jerked Maggie upright. The pounding was fierce. Outside, the thunderstorm still rumbled. Flashes of lightning danced nearby. Instantly, Maggie was on her feet. Disoriented from the druglike sleep she'd fallen into, she glanced at her watch. It was fifteen minutes since Shep had left.

"Open up!" a deep voice called. "FBI! Dr. Harper! Open up! This is the FBI!"

Hesitating, Maggie ran to the door. Should she open it? Where was Shep? He was late. Oh, Lord, why had she fallen asleep?

"Dr. Harper? Open up! This is the FBI. We've got a situation. You're in danger! Open the door now!"

Her heartbeat tripled in time. Dry mouthed, Maggie started for the bedroom, where her pistol lay, but looked out the peephole of the door as she passed. She saw a man dressed in dark blue clothes, a baseball cap that had FBI printed in yellow across the front. He was older, around forty-five, his dark brown eyes narrowed with tension. Should she open the door? Shep had told her emphatically not to.

"What situation?" Maggie yelled through the door.

"Ma'am! Your partner, Shepherd Hunter, is down! The terrorists got him. Open up! You're in danger! We have to protect you!"

Shep! With a moan, Maggie grabbed for the brass doorknob. Wait! Was she crazy? She wasn't following procedure! Jerking her fingers, she shouted, "What's the security code?" The FBI had a code set

up if something went awry and they needed to talk to
one another. Anyone could claim he was an FBI agent
and Maggie wouldn't know the difference. Knowing
the code ensured that the players were actually who
they said they were. Breathing hard, she waited, her
hands pressed against her breast.

"Alpha bravo whiskey!" the man shouted. "Now
come on! We've got a man down. We need you *now*,
Dr. Harper!"

The code was correct. Shakily, Maggie jerked back
the dead bolt. Next came the chain. She twisted the
knob. Before she could open it, the door was smashed
inward by the weight of a man's body. With a cry,
Maggie was thrown to the foyer floor, her breath
knocked out of her. Stunned, she saw two men leap
into the villa. One was dressed in a dark blue FBI
uniform from the waist up. The other man was in
civilian attire. Panicked, Maggie tried to scramble to
her knees to avoid his outstretched hand snaking toward her.

"No you don't, Dr. Harper." The man had a British accent, she noted numbly as he drew a gun and
pointed it in her face. "Now be a good girl and get
up. Now!"

The other man ripped off the baseball cap,
shrugged out of the dark blue shirt and turned to
them. Beneath the uniform he was wearing a short-
sleeved, crimson shirt. His hair was black, with gray
at the temples, his eyes dark green. He looked familiar, Maggie thought, as he smiled savagely in her direction. "How trusting you are, Dr. Harper." His accent was thick now and sounded Russian.

Confused and scared, Maggie watched as the one
with the Russian accent hurried to her bedroom,

where the aluminum attaché case sat in plain view upon the bed. "What? Who are you? You're not the FBI! How did you know the code?" And then, suddenly, Maggie recognized the man standing tensely at her side. He was a scientist she knew from conferences she'd attended for the OID. She'd heard him speak on anthrax epidemics a number of times. "Wait...you're Dr. Bruce Tennyson. From Britain. I—don't understand. What are you doing here?"

Chuckling, the man drew out a pair of handcuffs and pulled Maggie's hands behind her. "No, Doctor, we aren't the FBI and yes, I'm Bruce Tennyson. At your service."

"Shep?" Maggie asked, her voice cracking. "How bad is he wounded?"

"That was a lie, too, Doctor. Come on! You're going with us." He jerked a look over his shoulder at his friend. "Romanov?"

"Got it!" Alex Romanov called triumphantly from the bedroom. "Everything's here. The vial is here."

"Are you *sure?*" Tennyson snapped tensely as he pushed Maggie toward the door, his pistol jammed between her shoulder blades.

"Absolutely!" Romanov ran out to where they stood, grinning from ear to ear. "We got it!"

"Don't gloat yet, old chap," Tennyson said as he thrust Maggie ahead of him. "We've got to get out of here first. Let's go, Dr. Harper!"

Maggie jerked a look over her shoulder. The door of the villa was standing wide open. *Shep!* Oh, Lord, she'd done what he had said not to do! She'd opened the door! Now she was kidnapped. But how had they known the code? She'd never have opened that door if they hadn't given her the correct password. The pain arcing between her shoulder blades was intense as Tennyson jabbed her again, forcing her at a trot down the deserted hall toward the front of the building.

Romanov chuckled as he jogged beside her. "This is too sweet! We get the vial and the doctor. The FBI are going to be angry, eh, my friend?"

Tennyson grinned tightly as he jerked open the door that led outside to the stairs and the underground garage. "More than a little, Dr. Romanov. More than a little. Did you leave our calling card?"

"Of course," the Russian replied, hurrying down the stairs. Wind and rain whipped around them, the water making spots upon the crimson shirt he wore. "They'll know Black Dawn got to the anthrax and Dr. Harper," he gloated. "That other agent is going to be angry and in a lot of trouble. He left her wide open for the plucking...."

Six

Maggie sat shivering in the rear seat of the white van. The material of her blouse clung to her chilled flesh. She had gotten soaked in the downpour as they made a dash for the van, a vehicle, she noted, that looked exactly like that housing the FBI mobile headquarters. Her head spun with a hundred questions and no answers. She had to think!

She tried to steady her breathing. The driver and passenger side windows were tinted, making it impossible for those who passed by to see inside. Fear zigzagged through her as she studied the man who had joined them. Small and lean, he looked to be of South American descent. Something about his demeanor told Maggie he was a killer, not a doctor like she knew both Tennyson and Romanov to be. She still couldn't believe that Tennyson, who five years ago had been considered a leading expert on anthrax epidemics, was now stealing what he thought was DNA-altered anthrax for a far more deadly purpose.

Shaken, Maggie tried to see out the windows. The thunderstorm was gathering in fury, the rain sleeting almost horizontally, so she would see almost nothing. They passed the marina at a crawl, probably so they wouldn't garner attention. Where was Shep? Why had he been delayed? Her mind spun drunkenly and she glanced to her left, where the South American sat dressed in military fatigues, a pistol at his side. His feral-looking black eyes regarded her as if he were a hooded snake and she the prey, she noted, a shiver of terror running down Maggie's spine.

"Can't you at least uncuff me now? I'm losing circulation in my hands and arms," she pleaded to Tennyson, who sat ahead of her in the passenger seat. Romanov was driving, all his attention on the wet, flooded surface of the road as they headed toward the main route off Hilton Head Island.

Tennyson turned his head. "Juan, take the cuffs off Dr. Harper and put them back on when she's got her hands in front of her."

Maggie gulped as the man unwound like a lethally coiled snake. She leaned forward and turned her back toward him so he could reach the cuffs more easily.

"*Señorita,* do not think this is an invitation to try and leave," he warned her in a smooth tone.

Trying not to jerk away from his rough, hurtful hands as he unlocked the cuffs, Maggie groaned, then slowly eased her arms forward. As soon as she slumped wearily back in the seat, Juan loomed over her grasping her wrists to cuff them once more. When he had finished, he sat back down and smiled at her.

"You are a pleasant surprise, *señorita.* Dr. Tennyson did not think we could capture you alive. But here you are.''

Trying to think coherently, Maggie watched as the van turned onto the main route off the island. The thunderstorm was abating, the rain reducing in fury. Ahead, she could see the arc of the bridge to the mainland. Shep would come back to an empty villa. He wouldn't have a clue as to what had happened. Swallowing hard, she rasped, ''Bruce, how did you get the FBI code?''

Chuckling indulgently, he relaxed, turned his seat and gave her the kind of fond look a father might give an ignorant child. ''Dr. Harper…may I call you Maggie? You and I were always on pleasant terms as colleagues at those conferences around the world.''

Instinctively, Maggie realized the only way out of this situation was to lull them into thinking she wasn't going to try an escape. She was; at first opportunity, she planned to try and get away from them. But they didn't need to know that now. ''Yes…of course…call me Maggie.''

Smiling genially, Tennyson twisted his head toward Romanov. ''See? I told you so. She's one of us. She just doesn't know it yet.''

Romanov shrugged. ''We'll see….'' he said tensely as he pressed on the accelerator. They sped out of the storm and back into sunlight and a dry highway as they drove across the causeway.

Turning, Bruce smiled triumphantly. ''Well, it was rather easy, Maggie. What the FBI doesn't know is that we've got a mole inside their bureau. We have been given the daily change of codes ever since we started tailing you to get the DNA anthrax.''

''A mole?'' she gasped. ''Who?''

"*Señorita,* surely you do not think we're so stupid as to tell you?"

"She's just naive," Bruce chortled. "My dear Maggie with the beautiful red hair, we aren't going to divulge any names to you."

"Is that because you're going to kill me sooner or later?" she demanded. Fearing that they would, she turned her mind to escape plans. The van had three exits: the front passenger's and driver's doors and a double door at the rear. There were no side doors. It made escape impossible. Plus, her hands were cuffed, but Maggie knew she could manage with them bound if the opportunity to escape occurred.

"Oh, my, no," Bruce said in exaggerated horror. "Maggie…you're one of the world's top virologists." He preened a little and patted his chest confidently. "I'm the best in my country, Britain. Alex, as you well know, is at the top if his game in Mother Russia."

She glanced at the lethal-looking Juan. "And him?"

"Captain Juan Martinez is from Brazil, my dear. He's a part of Black Dawn, as well. You might think of him as your bodyguard and our protector." Smugly, Bruce smiled at his companions. "Although I must admit, we've all been through mercenary training over in Afghanistan with some of the best bioterrorists in the world. We pulled off a coup by getting you and the attaché case."

Sitting there, Maggie felt her heart ache, but not out of fear. She was thinking about Shep, what might have been and would probably never be, now. Despite their bickering and their problems, she loved him. She had to admit it to herself, because chances were she would soon be dead. It was just a matter of time. If there was any solace to the situation, it was that Shep had been gone when Black Dawn attacked. At least his life had been spared.

"And if my partner had been there when you came," she asked, "would he be here with me?"

"Him?" Bruce wrinkled his long, narrow nose. "Of course not. He's just a mule. A soldier. He doesn't have your knowledge, Maggie."

"No," Alex said with undisguised pleasure, "he would be dead."

Cold terror worked through Maggie and her stomach clenched painfully. Once more she tried to think, but it was so hard. She watched as Romanov took a route north on the mainland once they had crossed the two arcing spans of the bridge. "Where are you going?" she asked.

"You'll find out," Bruce said.

"You're kidnapping me. Why don't you release me? You've got the anthrax. Isn't that what you came for?"

Bruce gave her a grin. "Maggie, if I have my way, I want to extend an invitation to you to join us."

Stunned, she felt her mouth drop open. "What?"

With an eloquent shrug, Bruce said, "Why not? Think about it, Maggie. Black Dawn has fifty of the best and brightest academicians from around the world, all of whom are at the top of their game as virologists, microbiologists, physicists and biologists. We really aren't the threat I see written all over your face, my dear. We are a band of people who see our world sinking into absolutely destructive ways. We want to change that. And we can. We have amassed more brain power than any one nation could ever think of having. We've developed a plan, a global one, to get rid of this rotten, infected environment we are forced to live in. We want a peaceful world, Maggie. Not the world we live in now, which is full of hatred, prejudice and murder, attackers who get off from death sentences or well-earned prison terms. No,'' he said, his smile disappearing and his eyes narrowing as he gauged her response, ''we want to cleanse the world and start over. And we've got the knowledge and the means to clean our house.''

Her heart thumped in terror over his words. He was insane. They all were, as far as Maggie was concerned. But she didn't dare show her disdain for his ideas. ''By releasing the anthrax you intend to wipe out several populations?''

''Yes, worldwide,'' he murmured in a pleased tone. Waving toward the front window of the speeding van, he added, ''We tried it on Juma Indian Village in Brazil. It was a success. Fifty percent of the population died.'' His brows knitted. ''The only problem was that our anthrax lab exploded, attacked by a secret U.S. government force, and we lost all our hard work. The professor heading the project was also captured. Unfortunately, he's in U.S. custody at a prison near Washington, D.C.'' He pointed to the attaché case next to Juan's right leg. ''That's why we needed the freshly altered DNA anthrax. We had none of our own. Well, now that we do, we'll take it to our new lab facility over in Albania, which is well hidden in the mountain country, and we'll produce a lot of action in a hurry. Then we can move forward with our plan to try it on a major U.S. city. When that is successful, we'll have all our members fly to different cities around the world and start the epidemic.''

The fact that they did not currently have any anthrax to use on a city provided Maggie with some relief. She knew how fast anthrax could be made, however. Little did they know that what they had in that vial was only E. coli, not anthrax. But it would take them days after smearing it on petrie dishes to find that out, and that bought her time. As well as Shep and the FBI. *Shep!* Her heart twinged with pain again. How vital he was to her. Why hadn't she told him how she really felt about him? She was just as stubborn as he was when it came to waving a flag of truce and letting her real feelings be known. Meeting him again had undone her in the sweetest of ways. His kiss had opened up the beautiful treasures they'd shared before, treasures Maggie wanted now—and forever. But those hopes were now dashed. She was captured by a band of international terrorists who saw the world as one big infection that needed to be eradicated.

"So, you're going to fight fire with fire?" Maggie demanded throatily. "You see the world dominated by bad things, so you're going to let loose a bad bacteria to kill them off?"

"That's putting it crudely, my dear. Like cures like, does it not?"

"Not exactly," Maggie murmured tautly. "I agree we've got a lot of rotten qualities in the world today, but think of how many *innocent* people you're going to kill to get rid of those others."

"That's the price of a new world order, Maggie. We don't like it, but we can't separate out the rotting apples."

"Children are innocent!" she exclaimed hotly. "You three can sit here and condemn babies and children to a horrible, lingering death from this anthrax and say it's all right?''

Tennyson lifted his long, spare hands. ''Maggie, my dear, don't become upset over this. Look at the larger picture. The racial hatred, the prejudice, the murderers, thieves, rapists, the pedophiles—scum of the earth—will die, too. We want a world cleansed of such vermin.'' Tennyson's voice grew deep with conviction. ''I don't know about you, but I'm sick and tired of seeing our collective legal systems let off the damned criminals. Who gets hurt? We, the victims of crime, do. Criminals are given more rights than we are! Our systems of law stink. They have swung too far to protect the rights of cold-blooded murderers. Well,'' he said with satisfaction, ''that's all changing now. Members of Black Dawn have sworn a pledge to eradicate them all. We want a world order where people will be free from such vile and infectious trash!''

As she watched his green eyes glitter with fervor, Maggie tried to appear sympathetic. She had to somehow lull Bruce into thinking she was on his side. ''You know, you have a point.''

''Yes,'' Alex crowed, ''we do!''

''My own children,'' Bruce told her fervently, ''were here in U.S. schools for two years while I was working with your government. I was shocked at how degraded your public schools have become. My little Lisa was kidnapped by a local gang and held for ransom.'' He squeezed his eyes shut for a moment to get a handle on his emotions. Voice cracking, he said, ''And my boy, Christopher, who is only nine, was pistol whipped by another gang of boys after school as he waited for his bus.''

Anger shook the scientist's voice and he glared at Maggie. "Is it any wonder I feel the way I do? I paid the ransom and our daughter was returned to us, after being held for three days. She has changed so much since it happened. She was such a bright, beautiful ray of sunlight in our lives before. Now..." he lowered his voice, the pain obvious, "she is hyperalert, she trusts no one. She truly distrusts males—not that I blame my daughter—and worst of all, she shrinks away from me when I want to give her a loving squeeze or a hug to let her know I love her."

Sadly, he looked away. "My children have suffered gravely in your rotting country, Maggie. The worst thing is that, in both instances, no one was held accountable. The police to this day have not arrested anyone for those crimes. The experiences my children had are what drove me into working with Black Dawn. I want a *better* world for my children to grow up in. I want it free and clear of vermin. My wife is in anguish over what happened to our children. She is angry. And so am I. Those gangbangers got off scot-free!"

"I'm sorry," Maggie whispered. "I truly am, Bruce. I know our legal system isn't perfect—"

"Not anywhere near it," he snarled under his breath. Eyes glimmering, he said, "But now there's a way to change all this. I'm proud to be a part of Black Dawn. I feel badly that some innocents will lose their lives, but in the long run, we can eradicate the killers, the drug addicts, the thieves, the rapists and those who would stalk our children and abuse them. No, I want this new world order. My children have suffered enough!"

Maggie played along. She *did* feel for Bruce's chil-

dren. What a terrible experience they'd had in the
U.S. "You're right, Bruce, this is terrible. And your
children...I can only imagine how hard it was on you
and your wife at the time the incidents happened."

Miserably, Bruce nodded. "Now you see why I'm
backing Black Dawn. We *must* eradicate these inhu-
man species from the face of the earth. Black Dawn's
mission is to create a sane world once more. Not like
this world we live in." He jabbed his finger at the
aluminum case. "*This* is our way of doing it. When
it's all over, we can begin again. Laws can mean
something. An eye for an eye. None of this coddling
of prisoners. The death sentence will be imposed, and
believe me, it won't take twenty years to send one of
them to their rightful death, either."

Maggie nodded sympathetically, playing the game.
As they drove north, she had noted, sunshine and blue
sky had taken over once more. Traffic was at a min-
imum. She had to escape. How? Bruce was now treating her like she was already a member of Black
Dawn. "You know, what you say makes a lot of
sense," she forced herself to say. "Maybe you could
tell me more about Black Dawn, about your goals, as
we drive?"

Heartened, Bruce grinned. Alex perked up. Juan
gave her a distrusting look, however; he obviously
didn't believe her change of heart. The two scientists
did, but the Brazilian military officer saw right
through her. Maggie forged ahead anyway. She knew
that no help, no rescue was coming for her. It was up
to her to devise her own plan of escape.

"Maggie?" Shep's voice rang hollowly through
the villa. He dropped the pizza at the door, which he

had found wide open. Instantly, he pulled the gun from the holster beneath his left armpit. His heartbeat tripled in time. Thunder caromed around him, shaking the building in the aftermath. With his hand wrapped firmly around the butt of the pistol, he moved swiftly across the foyer, pointing the gun first right and then left. Nothing! No one. *Maggie! Oh, no. What happened?*

Breathing hard, Shep moved toward the left, where the two bedrooms were located. The attaché case was gone! Hurriedly, he searched the rest of the villa. Maggie was gone! Moving quickly back to the door, he examined the wood on the door frame. It showed no signs of a forced entry.

Jerking the cell phone out of his pocket, he made a call to the FBI. In a few minutes, they would come running to the villa, fully armed. Studying the entryway, he wondered what had happened. Maggie knew better than to open the door. Black Dawn had struck, he was sure. Walking back to Maggie's bedroom again, he rapidly searched it. On the dresser he saw a business card. Peering down at it, he felt his heart stop for a moment. On it was printed a caduceus— two snakes entwined around a staff. Only instead of the wings appearing in the symbol for physicians, the top of this caduceus held a globe of the world.

Shep's mouth went dry. He didn't dare touch it, for fear of smearing fingerprints that might be on it. It was Black Dawn's symbol.

Spinning around, he felt a cry of terror working up through his chest and into his throat. He wanted to scream out in rage, but forced himself to walk back to the living room and wait for the FBI to arrive. His heart hurt. Terror ate at him. He'd failed Maggie—

just as he'd failed Sarah. Closing his eyes, he sternly ordered himself to stop letting his wildly escaping emotions take over. He had to think! And think clearly.

Hearing the thud of booted feet coming down the outer hall, he met the FBI contingent at the front door.

The FBI team was composed of six men and women, all snipers carrying M-16 rifles that were locked and loaded. They were dressed all in black, including flak jackets and protective helmets. Their leader, Agent Bob Preston, halted. In his late thirties, he was about six foot tall, lean like a whippet, with sharp, alert eyes and a long, narrow face.

"Black Dawn has taken Dr. Harper and the attaché case," Shep told him. The looks on the faces of the FBI contingent told him they were all crushed by the news.

"But, how—" Preston began in a strangled tone.

"Maggie let them in," Shep breathed savagely, pointing to the doorjamb. "For whatever her reason, she let them in."

Preston studied the wood along the lock for only a moment, then he straightened and turned. "Bayard, Mitchell and Connors, do a door-to-door search. Canvas the area, starting with this floor. The rest of you, spread out. See if you can find anyone who might have seen something in the last thirty minutes around this building or the underground garage. Call the instant you hear anything."

The FBI agents scattered like a dark cloud of startled ravens, moving in all directions. Shep walked back into the villa, shoulders slumped with guilt and anguish. Preston followed him into the quiet confines and shut the door. He shouldered the rifle, his face grim.

"Dr. Harper knew not to let anyone in unless they had the code. That code was changed daily."

Unhappily, Shep nodded. "I was gone thirty lousy minutes. I didn't think Black Dawn would know where we were, because we changed our plans at the last moment." Raking his fingers through his dark hair, Shep cursed softly at his own misguided rationale. He led the agent to the bedroom. "There's a business card there, on the dresser. It needs to be dusted for fingerprints."

Nodding, Preston put on a pair of latex gloves, picked up the item and placed it in a secure plastic Ziploc bag. "No sign of a struggle?"

Looking around, his brows locked downward, Shep muttered, "Nothing's been knocked over. There's no evidence of blood splatters anywhere. Nothing else seems taken. Just Maggie and the attaché case..."

Preston sighed and moved back to the kitchen, where he laid his rifle down and took off his helmet. He pulled a radio from inside his flak jacket. "The good news is they couldn't have gotten very far."

"We need a lead. A break," Shep muttered, more to himself than to Preston. *Damn!* He'd left Maggie alone and unprotected. What was wrong with him? But, he had been *sure* she wouldn't open the door to anyone but him. Some kind of ruse had to have been used. She had to have been thoroughly tricked, because she wasn't a fool. And he was sure she'd have used the code. Rubbing his jaw, he waited until Preston got off the phone.

"Only your mobile HQ knows the daily code, right?" Shep demanded.

"Only them. I'm the one who chooses the password. We then send it out to you at 0800 each morning."

"*How* do you send it?"

"Scrambled. If you're thinking someone picked it up on the airwaves, there's no way it could have happened. That scramble is solid. No one to our knowledge has broken the encoding."

"Unless…" Shep began thinking slowly out loud. "Unless one of your people is a mole and slipped Black Dawn the code."

Preston's dark eyes sharpened. His mouth turned tight. "A mole?" he demanded scathingly. "I think you're feeling guilty over screwing this up, Hunter, and you're trying to pin Dr. Harper's kidnapping on the FBI. That isn't going to wash with us. Your theory is DOA."

Wrestling with his anger, Shep growled, "*No* agency is foolproof and you know it. The FBI has had its share of moles in the past, so don't try and sanitize that possibility with me. It won't work."

Preston's face whitened but before he could say anything, his cell phone squawked. Flipping it open, he growled, "Preston here…"

Shep saw the expression on the agent's face turn hopeful. Tensely, he waited until Preston was off the phone.

"What have you got?"

"Good news. Mitchell just interviewed a tourist staying here. She reported seeing a plain white van with tinted windows near the underground garage roughly twenty minutes ago."

"Did she see anyone?"

"Yes," Preston said triumphantly, "two men and

a woman. She described the woman as having red hair.''

Shep's heart squeezed. "Was she all right?"

Preston nodded. ''Yes, she said the woman had her hands bound behind her in what looked like handcuffs, but she appeared okay. She said they opened the rear of the van and hurriedly climbed in. The van left—'' he looked at his watch ''—around 6:45, give or take a few minutes.''

"Did she see the make of the van?"

Preston shrugged. ''No, she didn't. You know how women are about that. They never notice the make of a vehicle, just the color.''

"Damn!"

''Hold your horses, Hunter, we might have another break.'' Preston smiled a little. ''Did you know the bridge leaving the island has a camera trained on outgoing traffic? I'm going to contact the highway department and tell them to hold that piece of videotape for us. If there was a white van going across that bridge, then we know for sure they're on the mainland instead, and we can mount a search.''

Heartened, Shep said, ''Let's keep our fingers crossed.''

''You get down to the bridge,'' Preston suggested. ''There's a road on the right that leads to a small blue building where a security guard and the camera are located. Call me if you find anything?''

''In a heartbeat,'' Hunter promised, already out the door. As he hurried down the stairs, he barely took note that the thunderstorm was over. It was 7:00 p.m. They had another two hours of daylight, more or less, to try and spot that white van. The air was pungent with the odor of freshly washed pine trees as he loped through the underground garage to the sedan. Sliding in, he focused his mind as he drove out into the slanting, evening sunshine. First he had to contact Perseus. He had to let Morgan know what had happened. Shep's conscience ate at him as he punched in the Perseus number on his cell phone. What would they think of him botching this top event? Even worse, if Maggie was still alive, what would *she* think of him? He'd let her down, just as he'd let Sarah down.

As he sped along the rain-washed black asphalt houses and trees sped by him in a blur. Once out on the main route, Shep stepped on the accelerator. Speed was of the essence now. If that videotape revealed a white van going to the mainland, that was all he needed.

"Lookie here," the security guard, Jameson Curtis, said in a soft, Southern drawl. Dressed in dark-blue pants and a short-sleeved, light-blue shirt, he sat in his chair pointing to one of the television monitors as he ran the last hour's videotape on it. Scratching his balding head, he said, "Here's your suspect, Mr. Hunter." He punched the stop button on the VCR. Squinting his gray eyes, Curtis added, "And you can see the license plate on that van plain as day." He wrote the number down for Shep.

Nodding his thanks, Shep reached for his cell phone.

"We've hit gold," he told Preston, giving him the van's make, model and plate number. He heard Preston repeat the information into another phone plugged into the FBI agency, where the numbers would be run and the owner located.

"Wait one minute," Preston said.

Impatiently, Shep waited, staring at the television screen as he did so. The white van, which looked like an ordinary workmen's truck, had some scrapes and a dent on the right rear side, he noted. Slightly dusty, slightly used, it would blend into a stream of traffic with no problem.

"Hunter?"

"Yeah?"

"The van is registered to an auto rental place in Savannah—secondhand vehicles mostly. The man who signed the five-day rental is Bruce Tennyson. Does that ring any bells with you?"

"Hell, yes!" Shep exclaimed softly. His heart beat hard. "Dr. Bruce Tennyson is a British virologist who used to work for the U.K. on top secret projects that involved creating viruses for biological warfare situations. He disappeared, literally, five years ago after coming back from a two-year stint here in the U.S.A."

"And he's in Black Dawn?"

"The list I've got says he is. A Professor Valdemar identified him as one of the key leaders in the movement."

"Jackpot," Preston whispered.

"Send out a statewide APB on him. In the meantime, I'll rent a single-engine airplane from the Hilton Head airport and try and locate them from the air. A plane flying a hundred and fifty miles an hour can cover a lot of terrain in a hurry. Do you have any aircraft available?"

"Negative, we don't. That's a good idea. Rent a plane and keep in touch. We still don't know which way they went once they hit the mainland."

"I know. I'll start a search grid. I'll let you know more about it when I'm airborne so we can coordinate."

"Fine. Preston, out."

Flipping the phone case closed, Shep thanked the security guard and hurried to the car. Looking up at the sky, he eyed the thunderheads all around the island. Flying could get dicey in a small, fixed-wing aircraft without state-of-the-art instrumentation. It would certainly be seat-of-the-pants flying. Climbing into his car, Shep sped off toward the airport. On the way, he called Perseus again to keep them updated.

At the airport, he hurried to a small office that had Cessna printed on the door. Pulling out his wallet, Shep took out his flying license, the first thing they'd demand in renting him a plane. As he entered the small, cramped office, which reeked of cigarette smoke, a gray-headed man with a goatee and glasses looked up. He was tall and spare and dressed in a red T-shirt and jeans.

"Can I help you?"

"Yes," Shep said, laying his license on the counter between them. "I need to rent the fastest plane you've got."

Chuckling, his eyes crinkling, the man studied the license. "Well, Mr. Hunter, the only planes we have are Cessna 150s. We use 'em to teach folks how to fly."

"Are any available?"

"Just one."

"I'll take it."

"How long will you need it?"

"Twenty-four hours. I intend to do some flying in

the local area—maybe as far north as Charleston or down into the Savannah area.''

The man shrugged and pulled out an order form. ''You got a lot of thunderstorms right now, young fella.''

''I flew jets in the Air Force,'' Shep told him. ''I think I can handle some thunder bumpers.'' He was in a hurry, and the man seemed interminably slow. Shep tried not to convey his sense of urgency. He didn't want to cause a panic with the locals by alerting them of any danger in the area.

''Yes, sir, I guess you can.''

Just then, Shep's phone rang. He instantly opened it and answered, ''Hunter here.''

''Preston. We got another break. We sent out the APB, and a South Carolina state trooper just reported seeing a white van of that description going north on Interstate 95, heading in the direction of Charleston.''

Hurriedly, Shep grabbed an air map and spread it out on the counter. Fixing their position, he intently studied I-95 north of Hilton Head. ''I see the route.''

''There's a lot of hill country covered in pines up that way. And a lot of back roads. Dirt roads.''

''That's okay, it gives me a direction.''

''Listen, I'm coordinating for a helicopter out of Charleston, but the place is socked in with thunderstorms and they're grounded for now.''

''That's okay, I'll be going up into that area real fast.'' Shep glanced over at the old man, who was painstakingly filling out the form.

''Good. Once you get airborne, stay in touch.''

''Don't worry, I will,'' Shep promised.

Seven

The light, airy movements of the Cessna 150 felt good to Shep. Almost nurturing. He was always at his best when he was in the air. As he guided the white aircraft northward after taking off from Hilton Head island, the blazing western sun momentarily blinded him. He pulled aviator glasses from his shirt pocket and put them on. In the copilot's seat to his right lay his cell phone and an opened map of the area. Shep had been in a hurry to get into the air and had done a cursory walk-around of the airplane before leaping onboard and taxiing straight to the takeoff point.

Checking the radio, he found to his dismay that it wasn't working. Cursing softly he glanced over at his cell phone. At least he had that. He wouldn't be completely out of touch with Preston, who was now coordinating the entire search and capture effort from the Hilton Head police station.

Though grateful for any backup, Shep planned on being the one to bring these terrorists in. Grimly, he swung the aircraft over the I-95. It was thick with traffic between Hilton Head and Charleston. He took out his binoculars and checked out anything that looked white from his flying altitude of one thousand feet. By federal aviation requirements, no aircraft could fly lower than that unless landing or taking off. Shep had pushed the throttle of the single engine to the redline position. The Cessna 150 wasn't a race-horse. It puttered along in the turbulent blue sky that was gathering clouds and threatening more thunder-storms. The air was unstable due to the humidity and warmth coming in off the ocean. The Cessna atten-dant had warned him that another cold front was com-ing like a freight train from the west, bringing with it a thirty-degree drop in temperature. That was why the sky around him was suddenly alive with angry-looking stormclouds.

A little Cessna 150 couldn't take the wrenching updrafts and downdrafts of a thunderstorm, and Shep would be forced to fly around the huge formations or under them. The Cessna couldn't climb over ten thou-sand feet, so trying to rise above one of these huge, forty-thousand-foot cumulonimbus clouds was out of the question. No, he'd have to dodge and dart be-tween the mountainous masses instead. That, or fly real low, in which case he'd have rain to contend with, as well as fierce air pockets. If he got too close to the ground and got slammed by one of these big fellows, he'd be history. Downdrafts had knocked air-liners out of the sky at Dallas International Airport, and hundreds of people had died. Such a force would take his little aluminum Cessna and bend it like a pretzel in a matter of seconds, smashing him and it like a fly beneath a flyswatter into the muddy earth below.

Trying to keep the plane stable was nearly impossible, Shep found. Air pockets kept swatting the game little aircraft about, lifting or dropping it a hundred feet at a time, like a roller coaster. Anyone not used to flying would have been thrown long ago, but not Shep. He was used to powering hot chargers like the F-15 Falcon fighter, the premier jet of the Air Force. This constant bouncing around in the evening sky didn't bother him at all. It did make looking through binoculars tougher, however.

As he flew northward along I-95, his gut kept nagging at him. What if Tennyson didn't stay on the interstate? Shep knew he wasn't a stupid man. Tennyson would realize he would be safer and less likely to be spotted if he took a rural, less-traveled route. Playing his hunch, Shep grabbed at the open map and spread it out across the yoke in front of him. He devoted intense seconds to determining his present position. To his right was the Broad River and Port Royal Sound, a rectangular inlet on the South Carolina coast. North of the river mouth was Parris Island, the Marine Corps boot camp. There was also a marine air station on the island. To Shep's left was the small town of Switzerland.

How fast could the van be traveling? Shep tried to project the situation in his head. Speeds were supposed to be no more than sixty-five miles per hour, but just by eyeballing the traffic, he knew most cars were probably averaging around seventy-five. His little Cessna was pushing ninety-five miles an hour, which was close to its top speed. Calculating things in his head, he studied the map again. Tennyson would probably use a side road, if he could. Where

was the man going? What was his target objective?
Who was he going to meet? And where?

Blowing a puff of air from between his lips, Hunter
devoted half his time to flying the plane and the other
to studying the map of the area beneath him. He tried
to ignore his anguish and guilt over allowing Maggie
to be kidnapped. Was she all right? Was she dead?
What would Tennyson do to her? All the ugly
thoughts that came up only scored his aching heart
more deeply.

Cursing softly, he shoved his terror for Maggie
aside. He had to in order to think clearly. He barely
had an hour and a half's worth of light left. Trying
to search for the van at night would be impossible.
They would have to rely solely on the highway patrol,
which greatly lowered the possibility of finding Maggie at all. Being in the air was a huge advantage, but
the willing little Cessna simply didn't have the tech-
nical gear aboard to accomplish night hunts like a
military aircraft could.

Thirty minutes later, Shep diverted to a rural route,
Highway 17. It paralleled I-95 going north, but was
far less traveled. The sun was dipping closer to the
western horizon, the streamers of light now caught by
the gathering thunderstorms, which looked like or-
derly soldiers marching determinedly toward the
South Carolina low country. Feeling panicked because he knew he couldn't dodge the massive storm
front, Shep notched up the throttle to a hundred miles
an hour. Below him, the traffic on Highway 17 was
sparse. His gaze swept the route relentlessly. It was
fairly flat country beneath him, but thick with pine
trees. He had reached the Ace Basin National Wildlife
Refuge, drained by the Combahee River.

The whole area was a huge marsh, Shep realized.

The place must be alive with alligators, not to mention cottonmouth snakes that loved swimming in brackish water among rushes and reeds. The basin was ringed with millions of pine trees. It would be an excellent place to hide or meet someone.

Banking slightly to the left, Shep tipped the wing enough to see the highway ahead. Wait! His heart slammed against his rib cage. There! A white vehicle! Could it be them? Pulse pounding, adrenaline beginning to pump wildly through him, Shep tightened his hands around the yoke. He wanted to push the aircraft faster. The vehicle was miles ahead on a straight stretch and was heading for the bridge across the Combahee River. Wiping his mouth with the back of his hand, Shep glanced warily at the line of storm-clouds, now looming closer. In another fifteen minutes he either had to turn back toward Hilton Head or fly a helluva lot lower than a thousand feet. The massive black-and-gray, churning cumulus were almost upon him. Dark sheets beneath the clouds promised heavy, almost blinding rain. Either way, he could crash if he wasn't careful.

The aircraft inched closer and closer to the white vehicle. Taking the binoculars, Shep raised them to his eyes, his heart thudding violently in his chest. It was a white van! It *had* to be Tennyson! His hunch had been correct!

A violent updraft struck the Cessna. Shep instantly released the binoculars to take hold of the yoke to steady the plane. The aircraft was lurched to the right like a toy in the sky. The binoculars struck the opened cell phone lying on the copilot's seat.

"Damn" Shep snarled as he wrestled with the plane. Once he rode out the air pocket, he released the controls and reached out with his right hand. He shoved the heavy binoculars off the fragile cell phone. Picking it up, he pressed in some numbers. The screen did not light up. He tried it several times.

"Son of a bitch!" Again and again he tried it. Holding the yoke with one hand and opening the cell phone's battery case with the other, he checked to see if it was all right. It appeared to be. Once more he tried punching in the numbers to raise Preston. Nothing happened. Anger surged through Shep. The binoculars must have hit the device hard enough to loosen something inside it. Now there was no way to tell the FBI of his discovery.

Grimly, Shep thought about his options. There weren't many. He could land and try to find a phone to place the call. But where? Scanning the immediate area, he realized there was no airport available. Nor any suitable fields. He couldn't land in the marsh and he sure as hell couldn't land among the pines. Did he dare to stop following the van that he knew had Maggie on board? Tennyson could duck off the highway onto a lesser road and Shep could lose them completely. It was going to be dark in another half hour, at the most. What the hell could he do? Helplessly, he wondered how Maggie was doing.

"Bruce," Maggie said as sweetly as she knew how, "I have to go to the bathroom. Is there any chance we can stop?" She'd been able to lull Tennyson into thinking she was interested in joining Black Dawn. As a result, he'd ordered Juan to remove the strangling handcuffs. She now sat free and relaxed in the seat. Juan, however, did not trust her, and Maggie felt the soldier's dark, hooded eyes continuing to burn into her. She smiled as the doctor turned in his seat. It was nearly dusk, and they were surrounded by woods on both sides. It was a good place to try and make an escape. Maggie was scared. She wondered if they could hear her heart pounding raggedly in her breast.

There had been lightning and thunder around them for the last five minutes. Rain was starting to pound down upon them. It would be good cover if she got away. The thick stands of pines were less than a hundred feet from the highway and would provide enough cover for her if she was fast enough and smart enough. The rain, the whipping wind and the thunder would camouflage the noise of her escape *if* she made it to the trees. Maggie had no doubt that they'd track her down if possible. Still, they had to meet another contingent of Black Dawn in Charleston, so Tennyson might be torn between finding her and making the scheduled appointment.

Maggie knew that if she didn't escape they would take her with them—to Charleston and then overseas, to Albania. That was all she'd been able to get out of him thus far. She also knew that if she refused to join Black Dawn, he'd put a gun to her head and shoot her. It was clear to her now that Tennyson was a fanatic. Anyone who didn't join him was dead.

"Look at this!" Alex cried, and promptly slammed on the brakes. The van skidded slightly on the rain-slick asphalt.

Maggie peered through the windshield, past the beating wiper blades. The rain was so heavy that the blades couldn't do the job of helping with visibility. And suddenly, as if out of nowhere, dairy cattle were standing in the middle of the two-lane highway! To her left, she saw where a board fence had broken down, allowing a herd of at least forty guernseys to escape. They ambled contentedly about munching roadside grass or chewing their cud.

With a curse, Tennyson said, "Juan, you and I will get them out of the way. I don't want you blowing the horn, Alex, and alerting anyone. They're dumb animals, they'll move if we shout and wave our hands."

Braking to a stop, Alex nodded.

Juan quickly moved to the rear of the van, opened the doors and hopped out.

This was Maggie's chance! Swallowing against a dry throat, she waited until Tennyson and Juan had covered their heads with their jackets and started running toward the disinterested dairy cows. Looking around, she spotted a piece of pipe, about two feet in length and big enough to do damage, lying near her feet. The attaché case was there, too. Hands growing icy cold, Maggie watched Alex. His attention was fixed on the action taking place on the highway, which seemed to stretch endlessly across the flat land. There was no other traffic in sight.

Maggie tried to quell her fear. With a jerk, she reached awkwardly down for the pipe, grabbed it and straightened.

Alex turned at her sudden, unexpected movement. "Hey!"

It was the only word he got out of his mouth. Grasping the pipe with both hands, she swung it as hard as she could. The blow caught him just above the nose with a sickening thunk. Romanov groaned and slid against the door unconscious. Blood spurted from a cut across his brow where the pipe had connected.

"Oh, Lord!" Maggie grabbed up the attaché case and scrambled on shaky legs toward the rear of the van. Escape! She had to escape! The instant her feet touched the wet asphalt, she ran from the van toward the trees at an angle that would hide her from the terrorists line of sight. How long would it be before Tennyson found her gone? Seconds!

The rain slashed at her face. She ran openmouthed, hoping the harsh sound of her feet on the pavement wouldn't be picked up by them. No one was coming to her rescue. Maggie knew that. Slipping, almost falling, she leaped for the berm. Steadying herself, she saw the trees, less than fifty feet away. Oh, Lord, let her make it! Let her make it to safety! It was so hard to see where she was going! The rain pummeled her brutally, the drops icy and huge. Her hair quickly became a soaked mass around her neck and shoulders.

"Stop!"

Tennyson's shout was drowned out by a roll of thunder.

Maggie involuntarily flinched, but kept running. She heard the zing of bullets. Pistols were being fired—at her. Only twenty-five feet to go! The grass was slick. She nearly fell twice. Gasping wildly for breath, she stretched her short legs as far as they could go. Lightning flashed so close that it made the hair stand up on the back of her neck. Instinctively, Maggie dove for the trees.

There! Safety at last! Looking around wildly in the graying light of dusk, the rain slashing violently at her face and eyes, Maggie kept on running. Her lungs burned. Her breath was coming in ragged gasps. She again heard Tennyson's voice. Close! He was so close! Maggie knew he was strong and athletic and had a much longer stride than she. It would be no time before he caught up with her.

The trees swallowed her up. Brush grew in clumps

here and there, and thick brown pine needles carpeted the forest floor. Because sunlight didn't reach the earth in these massive groves of pines, the undergrowth was nearly nonexistent. She heard pistols being fired. Bullets sang by her head once again, some striking pines nearby. Flinching, she tried to shield her eyes with her free hand as she ran. Like shrapnel, the splinters could easily wound her or enter her eyes and blind her.

Running, her knees weak with fear and exhaustion, Maggie felt the attaché case numbing her wet, slick fingers. It was slowing her down. She had to get rid of it! Up ahead, she suddenly saw a clearing. What was it? Barely able to make it out through the thick veil of rain and the buffeting wind, Maggie tried to quicken her pace on the slippery pine needles. As the trees thinned ahead of her, she realized she'd reached a river. *A river!*

A plan came to mind. She jerked a look over her shoulder. The rain was so heavy that she couldn't see her pursuers. If she couldn't see them, they couldn't see her. Changing direction, she headed toward the muddy-looking ribbon of river. As she neared the marshy bank, she tossed the attaché case into the tall, dark reeds growing there. It promptly disappeared, swallowed up. Good!

Turning on her heel, Maggie headed back into the relative safety of the trees. She heard Tennyson shouting to Juan. They were to her left. *Good!* Somehow she'd evaded them, but Maggie knew it wasn't over by a long shot. Somewhere she had to find a place to hide. The land was becoming slightly hilly. Black rocks jutted out here and there. She had to hide! She knew Juan might find her. A trained mercenary, he was probably a ruthless hunter.

As she ran, Maggie thought of Shep. She loved him! She'd never stopped loving him, she realized. Would she be given a chance to consummate her love with him? To let him know how she felt about him? Running raggedly now, because she was out of breath and not used to this kind of physical stress, Maggie knew she had to push on or die.

Alex Romanov groaned. His hand went to his bleeding forehead. What had hit him? Blearily, he sat up and looked through the windshield soaked with rain. The dairy cows had gone back through the broken fence. Where were Bruce and Juan? Looking over his shoulder, he remembered that Dr. Harper had struck him and knocked him out. She was gone! *No!*

Thunder caromed around him. Reaching for his pistol from his shoulder holster, he realized that his friends must be out trying to find her. Just as he prepared to open the door, he heard a strange noise. It wasn't thunder. And it wasn't lightning. What the hell was it? Stymied, he peered through the rain-washed windshield. His mouth dropped open. There, coming out of the slashing, wind-whipped rain, was a small white-and-red airplane! To his amazement, it was trying to land on the highway where they were parked! It wasn't more than half a mile away from the van. What the hell was going on?

Gripping the pistol, Alex stared at the aircraft. What should he do? Was the pilot having engine trouble? Was it the U.S. government? An enemy? He wasn't sure, but he wasn't going to take any chances. Even if the pilot managed to land in this frightening thunderstorm, he was a dead man.

Sucking in a breath through tightened lips, Shep held the Cessna as steady as he could. Drafts from the thunderstorm were trying to wrench him up and down. For every downward pressure against the plane, he had to instantly compensate as he guided the lightweight aircraft toward Highway 17 below. And he knew that with every hundred foot drop in altitude toward that wet, slippery asphalt, the chances of him being killed were tripled. The storm raged around him. As it pummeled the aircraft the Cessna shuddered and bucked from side to side.

Shooting a glance at his altimeter, Shep saw he was less than two hundred feet above the roadway. A half mile ahead, he saw the white van. Grimly, he used his feet on the rudders to keep the plane on the glide path. The rain became worse. He could no longer see the van. He was trying to land this thing in the worst possible conditions known to pilots. It might work in an airliner, but not in one of these little aircrafts. The small plane was too lightweight, too responsive to every blast of wind, to every purging veil of rain that avalanched around him.

One hand gripping the yoke, the other on the throttle, Shep slowly cut his speed as the plane came closer and closer to the pavement below. Sweat popped out on his wrinkled brow. Shep's eyes narrowed to glacial ice. The road suddenly loomed up in front of him.

At the last second, a gust of wind slammed into the plane. It bobbled. The nose thrust upward.

No!

Jamming the yoke down to compensate, Shep saw the highway suddenly lunging upward at him. *Damn!* He'd overcompensated. Instantly, he yanked the nose up again. The asphalt still came at him, the Cessna's fixed landing gear crashing into the pavement. The plane bounced back into the air. Shep sucked in a breath. He steadied the plane and cut the engine. He jammed the throttle downward, shutting off the fuel supply.

The Cessna settled on the asphalt with a loud crunching sound. This time it didn't leap back into the air. The wind shoved it to the left, so Shep applied a strong left rudder to stop it from being blown off into the grass. He was down! Ahead, the veil of rain began to lift. Pushing on the rudder tips, he braked the plane, which came to a shuddering stop. Quickly grabbing his cell phone, he placed it beneath his jacket, then drew the Beretta out of its holster. As the rain curtain moved on past him, he saw that less than a quarter of a mile away the white van was parked in the middle of the road. Eyes narrowed and intense, Shep spotted a man in the vehicle.

Heart beating hard, Shep waited a moment to fix his position. There was no doubt that it was the Black Dawn van. So why was it parked there? He saw the dairy cows off to the side and the broken fence. Rapidly putting things together, he wondered where the other Black Dawn members were. This didn't look good. Had Tennyson stopped the van, taken Maggie out and shot her in the head, leaving her body in the woods that surrounded them? Heart aching, Shep wanted to deny that possibility. Maybe the cows had blocked their path? If so, why was the van still parked? It didn't make sense.

A flash of lightning overhead made Shep wince. The driver in the van still hadn't moved. The hair on Shep's neck went up in warning. Shep got out of the airplane with pistol in hand, the man would know he was an agent or someone who recognized the van. That was a giveaway. Yet Shep didn't like the odds. He saw another curtain of heavy rain approaching from his left. The tree line there was about a hundred feet away. He would use the cover of the thunderstorm to make it to the woods. And then he could watch and wait. Or at least try to buy time until he could figure out what was going on.

As the rain struck, Shep waited until the van disappeared behind its fury. Scrambling out of the plane, he launched himself toward the trees. All the while, as he sprinted, he listened for gunfire. Nothing. The rain soaked him instantly. Wiping the water from his face once he got inside the woods, Shep tried to steady his breathing. As the veil of rain lifted, he saw the van again. Only from this angle, he realized the back doors were thrown open and there was only one person in the vehicle. So what had happened to Tennyson? The woman who had seen Maggie taken had said there were two men.

Panicking at the thought that two of them had taken Maggie into the trees to kill her and leave her body, Shep turned and began jogging alertly toward the river, which he knew was less than a quarter of a mile away. As he jogged, he took note of his surroundings. The forest floor was covered with a thick mat of slick brown pine needles. He heard shouting—a man's voice. And then gunfire ahead of him.

Dodging behind one of the slender pine trees, Shep halted. He breathed through his mouth, the rain washing across his frozen features. Blinking rapidly, he looked around the trunk. Frantically, he tried to fix the sounds, but they were blurred and distorted by the thunderstorm rolling violently across land.

More gunfire. *To the left! Yes!*

With a curse, Hunter shifted and dug his toes into the soft, muddy soil littered with pine needles. They were chasing someone! He heard two male voices

drifting toward him from time to time. They seemed
to be moving away. If only the storm weren't roaring
around them! Other sounds were muffled so that Shep
couldn't get a good fix on where they were coming
from.

Running hard, he kept his gaze fixed to his right.
Somewhere in this pine grove were two Black Dawn
members. And if he was right, they were chasing
Maggie down like a dog. Had she escaped? She must
have! But how? His hopes skyrocketed. He held the
gun high in his hand as he raced among the trees.
Suddenly he tripped and fell. Slamming into the
ground, Shep groaned, rolled once more and leaped
back on his feet, barely missing a stride as he headed
at an angle toward the voices of the terrorists.

Inside his head, inside his wildly beating heart, he
prayed that Maggie was still free. He prayed that she
could outsmart them in this brutal thunderstorm, use
it to hide in, use whatever was around to keep her
safe from the murdering thugs. Because, as Shep
knew too well, if Maggie had escaped, and Black
Dawn found her, they would kill her on the spot.
There would be no mercy for the woman he knew he
loved with a passion that had never died.

As he continued to sprint through the grove, he
wasn't sure any longer if his eyesight was blurring
because of the slashing rain or because of his own
tears at discovering that he had never stopped loving
Maggie through all this time. He wanted a second
chance with her. Yet they were up against one of the
top terrorist groups in the world, one of the best
trained. Maybe Maggie's event riding would give her
a better sense of how to use the terrain as a friend,
as camouflage, than most people would. Maybe her
superb athletic condition could give her the edge she

needed to outrun these terrorists who wanted her
blood and her life.

Swallowing hard, Shep tried to steady his breathing
and keep up his ground-eating stride. When lightning
suddenly sizzled above him, the entire area lit up like
a million-watt lightbulb. Blinded momentarily, Shep
hit the ground hard. Air woofed out of his body as
he struck the earth. The thunder that followed milli-
seconds after the nearby lightning strike pounded his
body like a pugilist's punishing blow. Stunned by the
nearness of the strike, Shep slowly got to his feet.
Damn, that was too close for comfort. Raking his face
free of the water, he looked around, trying to separate
sounds of nature from the sounds of the terrorists.

Shouts! To his right. They seemed to be following
the course of the river. His gut told him to stay among
the trees and work at an angle away from the terrorists. If Maggie was escaping, she wouldn't use the
riverbank. Maybe she'd plunged in and tried swimming downstream? Shep was uncertain. Wiping his
eyes again, he headed off through the darkening
pines. Somehow, he had to pick up on Maggie before
Black Dawn found her. It was an impossible task, yet
Shep knew he had to try. He had to try because he
loved her, and he couldn't even think of life without
her vivid, vibrant presence lighting the darkness of
his unworthy soul.

Eight

Ragged gasps tore from Maggie's mouth as she labored to cross a stream that fed the river. The thunderstorm was violent, the rain slashing against her like icy, pummeling fists. Holding one arm up to protect her eyes from the furious wind whipping through the pines, she stepped into the stream. Maggie slipped. With a cry, she threw her arms outward, caught herself and then plunged forward. The bottom was muddy. How close were her pursuers? Gasping, she splashed drunkenly across the knee-deep stream, which was lined with tall green rushes. She grabbed a handful of them to steady herself. Instantly, they cut into her palm.

"Oww!" Maggie knew the reeds had to be handled carefully or they would lacerate her skin. Plunging her hand back into the water momentarily to wash away the blood, she wished she was taller. The rushes

swatted heavily against her as she clambered up the
bank on the other side.

A flash of lightning sizzled overhead. Maggie
crouched, then dropped to her hands and knees. It had
been so close! Almost instantly, thunder followed in
its wake, reverberating through her as if she were a
drum being struck. Hanging her head, the water drip-
ping off her nose and chin, she tried to orient herself.
Tennyson was probably still hunting for her along the
river, but she couldn't be sure. She *had* to find somewhere to hide. Lifting her chin, she peered through
the darkening forest. The flat land was swelling gently
in a series of knolls, with more rocks jutting out here
and there. Maybe, in the coming darkness and the
overhang of one of those large, black boulders, she
might be able to wait out her pursuers.

Rising on rubbery legs, Maggie realized she'd
pushed her body to its limits. She desperately needed
a fifteen minute rest to fuel back up for another run.
The sheets of rain eased as she cautiously looked
around. *Wait!*

A cry nearly tore from her. Was she seeing things?
The dusk was deep, and there were so many shadows,
so many things that resembled a stalking enemy. She
quickly knelt down in order to be less of a target.
Eyes narrowing, she gulped in unsteady breaths of air.
Maggie gripped the wet, needle-covered ground to
steady herself. *There!* Yes, she saw movement! *But,
who?* It wasn't near the river; quite the opposite. Was
one of the terrorists scouting inland for her? It was
growing so dark. If only she could see better!

Just then, another bolt of lightning lit up the dusk,
and Maggie's eyes widened enormously. There, no
more than two hundred feet from her, moving from
tree to tree, pistol held up and ready, was Shep! How

could it be? Was she seeing things? Was she making
this up because she knew she was going to die? Her
mind froze and her heart swelled wildly. It *had* to be
Shep! He was real. He *had* to be!

Rising unsteadily, Maggie wanted to call out to
him, to get his attention, but she didn't dare. If Shep
could hear her, so could her enemy. Sliding unsteadily
away from the stream, she finally found purchase and
broke into an erratic trot in his direction.

Something told Shep to look to his right. His lips
parted as he saw a dark figure running toward him.
Maggie! It was Maggie! She looked like a drowned
rat, her hair a sleek dark ribbon against her skull, her
clothes muddy, soaked and clinging to her skin. Her
eyes were huge with terror, her mouth open in a silent
scream. But she was all right! Shep turned on his heel
and headed directly toward her with long, loping
strides.

Lightning flashed as they drew close to one another. Shep controlled his desire to forget the dangers
and just hone in on Maggie. He knew he couldn't
resist touching her, though. Reaching out those last
few inches, he curved his left arm around her sagging
shoulders.

"Oh, Shep!" Maggie sobbed as she fell against his
tall, hard frame. "You're here! You're here!" She
gulped unsteadily and felt him press her hard against
his chest in a protective gesture. Clinging to him, she
found herself half crying, half laughing.

"Shh!" he rasped against her ear. Shep had
dragged her against him and located a large pine tree
to hide behind. Maggie felt so warm and soft against
him. He felt her fingers digging convulsively into his
shirt and chest as he guided her down between his
opened legs. They crouched together, using the tree

as a natural cover and support, protecting them from prying, unseen eyes.

Bringing his other arm around her, and making sure the pistol was pointed away, he embraced her closely and just held her. She was trembling badly and shivering from cold and shock. Pressing kiss after kiss against her wet hair, ear and cheek, he whispered harshly. "It's going to be okay, Maggie. Lord, I thought you were dead. I thought the worst…. I'm so glad you're alive, so glad…." He was blinded momentarily by a wave of emotion surging up through him as Maggie's hands moved around his neck. When she raised her chin, however, he saw the terror, the need, in her haunted hazel eyes. Shep would do anything to ease the fear from Maggie's eyes. Leaning down, he groaned her name and put the pistol aside. In one movement, he framed the cool, wet skin of her face, and kissed her. As his mouth closed over hers he felt her quiver beneath his warm, exploratory onslaught. Their mouths met hungrily. Almost violently. She tasted warm and alive. She tasted of life. He could feel her shivering in his arms, her mouth eagerly taking his and returning his wild, unexpected kisses with equal ferocity and need. Maggie was here! In his arms! She felt so damned good in his arms, like a wet, trembling puppy ecstatic at seeing his favorite human once again.

Tearing his mouth from hers, Hunter gazed deep into her tear-filled eyes. She looked so helpless in that moment, but Shep knew differently. With shaking fingers, he tried to wipe some of the rain away from her forehead and cheek. It was then that he realized she was crying. Probably out of sheer relief that she had not been abandoned by him, after all.

"How—" Maggie sobbed. She slid her hands over

his face, the prickle of his beard feeling wonderful to her chilled fingers. "How did you find me?" Her voice cracked again, and she couldn't help sobbing openly. The sense of relief was profound within her. "I didn't think anyone would find me...."

Gently, he smoothed the rainwater from her flushed cheek. "I wouldn't stop until I did, brat. Not ever..." His deep voice shook with emotion. Picking up the pistol, Shep angled his back against the tree. For a moment they were safe. They were talking low, and the rain, wind and thunder would certainly hide their whisper as they huddled for warmth in one another's arms. Absorbing her presence, his long, powerful thighs like brackets supporting Maggie in the downpour, he felt some of his guilt dissolving.

Choking back her tears, Maggie pressed her cheek against his shoulder. "Just hold me, Shep! Oh...just hold me. I'm so tired...so weak...." But he was feeding her with his incredible strength, she knew. Just being able to cling to Shep as the darkness fell was wonderful. The way he soothed his hand across her shaking shoulders made her feel hope. Finally, after a few minutes, Maggie lifted her head and looked up at his dark, familiar features. Though he held her closely, his gaze was darting alertly around them. She felt tension sizzling through his body and knew he was doing what he did best as a mercenary. Never had Maggie felt as safe, as protected, as now.

"How..." She managed to croak, her fingers sliding against his hard jawline. "How did you find me?"

He glanced down at her for just a moment before continuing to scan the forest. No place was safe as long as those three Black Dawn members were hunting them. "A lot of luck. A woman going to her car in the garage at the villa saw you being taken away

by two men. She described the van. We got a real
break when we found out there's a highway camera
at the bridge leaving Hilton Head. The security guard
ran the video back, and we got the van's make and
license plate number.''

Amazed, Maggie sank more deeply against him.
She felt Shep take her full weight. How good it was
to be held by him! ''And you followed us?''

He smiled grimly. ''I rented a plane from the island
airport and flew north. A highway patrolman saw the
van and reported it. I flew north following I-95, until
I found you.''

Her eyes widened. ''You were in a plane? In this
storm?''

His mouth flexed. ''I landed that sucker on the
highway a quarter of a mile from where the van's
parked.''

Amazed, Maggie stared up at him. ''That must
have been right after I escaped! Did they shoot at
you?''

Tightening his arm around her, Shep kissed her
cheek. Very slowly, the storm was moving to the east.
The rain was lessening, too. His lips near her ear, he
said, ''No. There was one man in the van, just sitting
there. I used the rain as cover to leave the Cessna and
make a run for the woods.''

''Oh...'' Maggie sighed and closed her eyes. ''I
brained him with a piece of pipe. His name is Alex
Romanov, Shep. I knocked him out and escaped out
the back of the van. There was a whole bunch of cows
on the road. That's why we stopped. Bruce Tennyson
and a Brazilian soldier named Juan left the van to
shoo them off the road. I took a chance....'' Maggie
shivered violently at the memory of her bold escape.
Pressing her face against his damp clothing, she

sobbed, "I was so scared…. I knew if they caught me, they'd kill me. Tennyson's a fanatic. I lulled him into thinking I'd join Black Dawn. That's why he took the handcuffs off me. I had to take a chance to get away when we got stopped by the cows." Opening her eyes, Maggie looked up at him. "I've never been so scared in all my life, Shep. This made event riding look like pabulum in comparison. I was sure they'd find me and shoot me."

Grimly, he grazed her wet hair with his fingers. "You're the bravest woman I've ever met, brat. There's not many that would have risked what you did."

Sniffing, Maggie wiped her nose and tried again to remove the tears from her eyes. "I just kept thinking, Shep…remembering the kiss we shared in Savannah, remembering all the good times we had together…and I didn't want to die. Tennyson is planning to meet another contingent of Black Dawn in Charleston, at a place known as the Kemper Plantation. And then we were all going to board a plane at the airport and fly to Albania. There are ten other Black Dawn members waiting for Tennyson to get to Charleston."

Nodding, Shep smiled warmly down at her as he slid his hand behind her head. "Maggie, what we have together, as flawed as it is, is good. You just hold on to that, okay? I'll get us out of this or die trying."

Trembling, Maggie absorbed his tender touch and the undisguised warmth and love she saw glittering in his narrowed eyes. *Love! Yes.* She wasn't going to lie to herself any longer about how she felt toward Shep—had always felt but had denied it—until now. Gulping, Maggie whispered, "We've got to get out

of this jam, Shep. I want a second chance with you.
You hear me?''

His mouth twitched in a bare smile. ''Brat, you're
my life. No matter what happens from here on out,
we're going to work as a good team. I'm going to try
and listen to you and not just take over like I usually
do. I've learned my lesson. Okay?''

How wonderful those words sounded to Maggie!
Jerkily, she nodded. The evening was cool in the
wake of the storms and she shivered every now and
then even though she was in Shep's powerful and
protective embrace. ''You're probably mad as hell at
me for opening that door to the villa,'' she whispered
apologetically. In bits and pieces, she told him what
had happened. She saw Shep's brows move up in surprise.

''They had the *code?*''

''Yes!'' Maggie whispered fiercely. ''Believe me,
that's the *only* reason I opened that door, Shep! Tennyson said there was a mole in the FBI feeding them
information. That's how they got their hands on the
password.''

Shep cursed softly. He moved slightly, his legs
starting to grow numb. ''Preston needs to know this,''
he muttered darkly.

''How? I mean, we're literally out in the middle of
nowhere here, Shep.''

''Not quite, brat. When I was flying in to land on
the highway, I spotted a dairy farm off to the right,
about a mile from here. It's on the other side of the
road where they parked the van. I hate to involve the
locals in this mission but we haven't much choice. If
we could get to the farmhouse, I could make the necessary calls.''

"But…what about Black Dawn? How are we going to get across that road?"

Easing upward and taking Maggie with him, Hunter rasped, "Very carefully." Pushing against the tree, he stretched to his full height. Maggie seemed diminutive against him, yet she had the heart of a courageous fighter. How many other women would have done what she had to escape? "Maggie the Lionhearted," he whispered in her ear. "Come on, let's go. Follow me closely. Keep your hand on my waist belt, okay? If I suddenly drop to my knees you drop too. Understand? And if you hear something, jerk on my belt and we'll go hit the deck together. This storm is moving on. Pretty soon it's going to be very quiet, and that's when they'll hear us moving around."

Her heart beginning to beat hard with fear once more, Maggie nodded. But she also felt a warm glow at Shep including her, asking for her help on this mission. Now they were really a team. The words *I love you* were almost torn from her lips as she wrapped her fingers around his belt.

Shep had been right. Within minutes, the storm moved toward the coast. In its wake the darkness was so thick they had to move slowly from tree to tree, their hands outstretched to find the next one. More than once Maggie tripped over unseen rocks and stumps. Her grip on Shep's belt stopped her from pitching onto her nose. He kept his stride short for her sake. She was amazed at how silently he moved. His body seemed boneless in comparison to her awkward, stumbling movements. Maggie tried to tell herself that he was used to such danger and had overridden the adrenaline rush to think clearly. She hadn't.

From time to time, she heard Tennyson's voice echoing eerily through the woods. And each time, they'd drop to their knees and wait. Each time, Tennyson's furious voice seemed to come from the river. As they neared the highway, Maggie heard Alex's thick Russian accent calling out for Tennyson. She and Shep both froze, slowly kneeling on the wet needles. Frightened, Maggie realized suddenly how close they'd come to the van! Gulping, she tried to get a grip on her escaping terror. Her night vision had adjusted now, and she could just make out the outline of the van against the dark specter of pine trees on the other side of the highway. When she saw the stabbing beam of a flashlight, she froze. Her breath jammed her lungs.

Shep gripped her hand and pulled her up. ''Come on!'' He saw the man with the flashlight heading away from the van toward the river. Now was their chance to cross the road!

Surprised, Maggie was wrenched upward. She hurried to keep up with Shep's lengthening stride. He was going to cross the highway in plain view of Alex! Was he nuts? She didn't have time to ask. They ran hard, down the slope to the berm and then quickly across the wet asphalt. On the other side, Shep led her to the break in the fence the cows had made earlier.

Gasping, her heart wildly pounding in her chest, Maggie felt herself pulled up the slight incline. They were once more inside the relative safety of the pines. *Good!* Her terror subsided a little as they slowed their pace. With night vision, now, they could see the silhouettes of trees so they wouldn't run into them. Shep kept his hand wrapped tightly around hers. Within minutes, they broke out of the pines into a meadow, where the dairy cows were contentedly munching grass or lying down for the night.

"There!" Maggie gasped, and pointed to their left. "Lights!"

Shep halted. He was breathing easily, but he heard Maggie's noisy gasping and knew he had to wait and let her catch her breath. Taking her in his arms, he realized they were targets standing out in the middle of the grassy meadow. "That's the farmhouse," he told her raggedly. Giving her a gentle squeeze, he said, "Can you walk? We've got to keep moving."

Nodding, Maggie absorbed strength and warmth from his embrace. "Yes, let's go...."

Sometimes they walked through the short, wet grass and sometimes they jogged. Maggie kept staring at the lights of the farmhouse in the distance. It appeared so far away! A mile? Or more? She often glanced across her shoulder as they moved silently from one pasture to the next. Each was rectangular and fenced off with white board fencing. They would crawl beneath the lowest board to avoid detection. The cows would lift their heads, stare at them and then return to eating, as if they instinctly knew Maggie and Shep did not pose a threat to them.

The farmhouse was on a knoll surrounded by stately, ancient live oaks. As they hurried up the graveled roadway, a dog began barking. Maggie's heart thudded with fear. She felt Shep's hand tighten momentarily around hers to reassure her. When the front door of the house opened, Maggie saw a man with silver hair come out and look in their direction. The dog at his side appeared to be a collie. It was barking nonstop.

Shep mounted the steps of the porch and halted in front of the man, who appeared to be in his sixties. He had a pinched face, weathered by outdoor life and hard work. Dressed in a pair of coveralls, his spec-

tacles resting low on his narrow nose, he put his hand
on the dog to silence her.

"What do you want, stranger?" the old man demanded.

Shep had already put his pistol away because he
didn't want to frighten the man. "I'm Shep Hunter. I
work for the FBI." He drew out his badge case and
held it up for the man to appraise. "We're in urgent
need of a phone. May we come in and use one?"

"Elmer?"

The woman's voice drifted out the opened door.
Maggie moved to Shep's side.

"Eh? Oh, it's some police people out here,
Trudy...." Handing the badge case back to Shep, he
asked, "There's trouble out there?"

Shep nodded. "Yes. We won't stay long. We just
need a phone, Mr....?"

"Elmer Hawkins." He turned to his wife, a thin
woman with short gray hair, wearing jeans and sweat-
shirt. "This is my wife, Trudy. Trudy, let 'em in.
These young folks are in trouble. They need the use
of our phone."

Shep nodded his thanks as the farmer told them to
follow him. Standing out on the porch made them all
targets. He breathed a little easier when the door
closed behind them.

Trudy clucked her tongue. "Ya'll are soaked like
a bunch of river rats." She smiled warmly and said,
"Come on, come to the kitchen. Let me get you
something warm to drink?"

"No, ma'am.... Thanks, but I need to get to a
phone," Shep said.

Trudy pointed off to the right of the shining cedar
foyer. "Right in there, in the living room, on the lamp
table next to the couch." She turned her attention to

Maggie. "You look cold to the bone. Let me get you a coat?"

Maggie smiled weakly. She had wrapped her arms around herself, but her teeth chattered no matter what she did to stop them. She knew she was slightly hypothermic. "Yes. That would be wonderful, Mrs. Hawkins. Thanks so much...."

"Go join him," Elmer said. "Trudy, I'll get these young people some dry jackets. You go make 'em some hot tea. This ain't a night fit for man or beast."

Grateful beyond words, Maggie walked quietly into the old, antique-filled living room. The furniture was all Victorian. Fresh flowers sat on a sideboy. The television was turned to a game show, but the sound was muted. Shep was using the phone, his voice low as he spoke intently to the person on the other end. Maggie didn't want to sit down on the furniture, upholstered in a lovely floral fabric, and get it sopping wet. No matter where she walked, she was leaving footprints. Her shoes were soaked. Shivering, she stood close to Shep and listened to him talk to Preston.

Elmer came back first. "Here," he told her in a whisper, "put this on. This is Trudy's warmest jacket."

"Oh, thank you," Maggie said with a broken smile. It was a fleece-lined, dark-blue garment with a waterproof outer shell. The moment she shrugged into it, she felt a modicum of returning warmth. Elmer put a black, rainproof jacket over the couch near where Shep stood talking.

"Here you go, my dear," Trudy said quietly as she brought in a tray holding two mugs of hot, steaming tea. "I put a little honey in it for ya'll. Hope you don't mind," she set the tray on the coffee table.

Picking up the rose-colored mug, she handed it to Maggie.

"Thanks so much," Maggie whispered, sliding her icy fingers around the warm, sleek surface of the mug. "You have *no* idea how wonderful this feels to me." Her teeth had stopped chattering now and she blew across the surface of the steaming, gold-colored tea to cool it a little. Sipping it, she felt fingers of warmth stealing down her throat and loosening the tightness in her stomach. The tea was herbal, and the sweetness made her smile. "This is wonderful," she told Trudy gratefully.

Pleased, Trudy touched her short, gray hair with pride. "It's my grandmother's recipe, you know. Chamomile with hops. You look a little shaken, dear. I thought a tea that would soothe your nerves was in order."

Laughing softly, more out of relief than anything else, Maggie felt some of the terror leaking away with each sip of the tea. "You're so sweet, Mrs. Hawkins. Letting us come in, two strangers out of the dark of the night...that's so very kind of you."

She nodded and fussed over Maggie, saying, "You're going to catch your death of cold, my child." She touched Maggie's limp, wet hair. "Can you stay here?"

"No," Shep said in a growl as he placed the phone back into the cradle. He glanced apologetically at the farm couple. "We need to keep moving."

Shep saw the terror in Maggie's eyes return as she gripped the mug to her breast, her hands wrapped tightly around it. Picking up his own mug, he sipped the hot tea with relish. "All the law enforcement authorities have been alerted," he told Maggie. Then, turning to the couple, he continued, "What I need now, Mr. Hawkins, if you've got it, is a vehicle and a cell phone. We need to get out of here and head toward Charleston. Do you have a car we could borrow?''

Trudy smiled and slid her arm around her husband's waist. ''Why, we have a truck you could use, Mr. Hunter. Would that do?''

''Anything will do,'' he assured them fervently. ''And if there's any damage to it while we use it, the government will pick up the tab for any repairs.''

''Oh,'' Trudy said, ''that's good. Hold on, I'll get the keys....'' And she hurried from the living room.

''What should we do, Mr. Hunter?'' Elmer asked worriedly. ''Any possibility this trouble that's obviously stalking you might make its way here?''

''I doubt it. But if anyone comes around asking questions, pretend you know nothing. Chances are, no one will harm you. They're looking for us. If they can't find us within a certain amount of time, I'm sure they're going to leave to get to their next destination. If they do come, just play it cool and dumb.''

Elmer smiled a little and rubbed his lean jaw. ''Dumb I can appear.''

Maggie laughed a little. ''You are far from dumb, Mr. Hawkins.''

Chortling, Elmer said, ''Well, now, you know how city folks look down on us dumb-as-sticks country folks.'' His blue eyes sparkled with mirth. ''Don't worry about us, little lady, we'll be fine.'' He turned when Trudy came back into the living room, holding a set of keys toward Shep.

''Which one did you give 'em?'' he asked his wife.

Trudy smiled a little. ''The three-quarter-ton truck. You think that tank will get them safely to Charleston?''

With a pleased chuckle, Elmer nodded sagely. "That truck is five years old, Mr. Hunter, but like my wife sez, it's a tank. That thing is the closest you'll come to protection. It will withstand a lot of damage and give better than it gets if you folks get into a jam."

Shep nodded. "I've got more luck than I deserve, Mr. and Mrs. Hawkins." He held up the keys and smiled in their direction. "When this is all over, we want to come back and thank you for your help. Without it, we'd be in big trouble." He also told Elmer about his cows breaking down the fence near the highway. "Right now, they're back inside your pasture and bedded down for the night. But I would look to repair that soon."

"Thanks for letting us know," Elmer said.

Trudy traded a smile with her husband. "Go out the back, through the kitchen, Mr. Hunter. Put this coat on first. You need to get warm, too. The garage is attached. Just go down the steps to the right. The truck is in there with our sedan."

Maggie reached out and gripped Trudy's long, thin hand. "You're both lifesavers. Thanks *so* much!"

"Ya'll just be real careful out there," Elmer drawled.

Shep shook the man's hand and thanked both of them for their courage and help. Without them, they'd still be shivering cold, with nowhere to turn.

Maggie hurriedly followed Shep, taking the concrete steps two at a time. A light automatically came on as they entered the garage.

"This is good," Shep growled. The huge, bright red truck stood there looking like a warhorse in full armor. "We got lucky. This truck can take a helluva beating and keep on running."

Climbing into the passenger side, Maggie met his eyes as he made himself comfortable. "Do you think there will be trouble?" Her fingers shook as she fastened the seatbelt.

Slamming the door shut, Shep started the engine. The truck growled to life, trembling around them. "I don't know. This truck has a big engine. We might need it." He glanced over at her as he prepared to back out of the garage. "If we get into trouble, you get down on the floor, understand?" Shep was damned if he was going to lose Maggie now that he'd just found her.

Licking her lower lip, Maggie whispered, "Don't worry, you won't have to tell me twice." She saw the set look of Shep's features. This was the man she loved. Would they be able to make it out of here? To escape Black Dawn? Shivering, she wrapped her arms around herself as Shep eased the big, hulking pickup carefully out of the garage.

"Are the police on their way up here?" Maggie demanded.

"Yes, but it's going to take time. We're thirty miles from the city." Moving the truck down the graveled driveway in the dark, he turned toward the highway. "Until then, brat, we're on our own...."

Nine

Shep drove without lights as they crept down the muddy, dark road toward the highway. All around them, they could see flashes of lightning from storms that had gone by and were heading toward Charleston, and those that were still looming over them to the west. He glanced at Maggie. She was making sure her seat belt fit snugly, for safety reasons.

"Take my pistol," he said, handing it to her. "I'll do the driving, you do the shooting. You're the pistol expert."

At last Shep was treating her like an equal, as if she was a valuable part of their team. Quirking her lips, Maggie grinned widely and teased, "Wise choice. Between the two of us, I'm the pistol shooting champion here." She glanced at him as she checked the gun and snapped off the safety.

"In this bag," he said, pointing between them, "are extra clips of ammo."

Shep's eyes narrowed as he studied the road ahead, which disappeared between the two stands of pines. "Be on guard," he warned her in a deep voice. "Those terrorists could be waiting for us down there." Tightening his hands around the wheel of the growling truck, he forced himself to breathe in and out. It was only a quarter of a mile to the highway. Elmer had said the road joined the highway near the bridge. That meant they were behind the van and the Cessna. Were the terrorists still looking along the river for Maggie? Had they returned to the van? Had they already left for Charleston? Hunter knew his and Maggie's lives hung in precarious balance and there were no ready answers.

Maggie's eyes widened as they crept forward. Her fingers were icy cold on the cool metal of the pistol. The thought of using it to kill someone sickened her. She loved target shooting precisely because it was sport and didn't kill or hurt anything. Feeling the tension reverberating through Shep, she spontaneously reached out and gripped his forearm.

"Listen, no matter what happens, Shep, I want you to know—"

Bullets suddenly hammered the truck. Maggie screamed and threw up her hands to protect her vulnerable eyes from the shattering windshield. Hundreds of pieces of glass blew in on them.

"Son of a bitch!" Shep jammed his foot down on the accelerator. The pickup truck roared like a wounded bull, its rear end slewing from side to side on the slippery mud of the road, until it gained purchase and lunged forward. He saw winking red-and-yellow lights of gunfire from both sides of the road. Aiming the nose of the truck through the fiery gauntlet, he saw Maggie begin to fire back. More lead slammed into the truck. The bullets sang past his head. He ducked and kept his gaze glued on the road.

The instant the pickup hit the asphalt of the highway, Shep jerked on the lights and swung it heavily toward the bridge. All the firing was behind them. *Good!*

Gasping, Maggie jerked an empty clip out of the pistol and jammed in another one. "You okay?" she cried. The wind was shrieking in through the windshield, which now had three huge, gaping holes.

"Fine. You?"

"Yeah…okay…."

Shep drove like a madman. They careened up on the bridge that crossed the river. The pavement was still wet, and the pickup, thanks to its superior weight, held the road even though she could see they were shrieking along at a hundred miles an hour.

Maggie twisted around. She saw lights suddenly switch on behind them. It was the van, she realized with a sinking feeling. "They're following us, Shep. Oh, Lord…"

"Get on the cell phone," he ordered her tightly. "Punch in this number…."

With trembling hands, Maggie did as she was told. Once it rang, she handed it to Shep.

"Yeah, Preston, it's me. Listen, we're in trouble. We're heading toward you. We just crossed the bridge over the river." He gave the make and model of the pickup. "The van with Black Dawn is in pursuit. What can you send our way to help us? We've got one pistol against the semiautomatic and automatic weapons they're carrying."

The lights from the truck stabbed the darkness. It was a lonely road with no traffic to speak of, hemmed in by pines on each side. It was a corridor to Shep, another gauntlet. He kept his gaze peeled for any back roads he could take to throw Black Dawn off their trail.

Maggie heard the tightness in Shep's voice as he spoke into the phone. She kept looking back, but didn't see the van's headlights—yet. The set of Shep's face scared her. Despite the darkness, the illuminated panel on the dashboard outlined his hard, rugged features like glacial ice. She heard the disappointment in his tone. He flipped the phone closed and handed it back to her.

"Preston is going to try and get a helicopter out of the Marine Corps air station on Parris Island. No promises, though, because they're ringed by thunderstorms. Damn..."

"How far until the state police can meet us?"

"Another twenty miles," he said flatly. Up ahead, he saw a dirt road. "Hang on," he warned her, and he slammed on the brakes. The tires squealed in protest, and the truck swung heavily from side to side as they slowed.

Maggie was holding on with both hands, gripping the seat and the door. "What are you doing?"

"Trying to lose them," he grunted, and swung the truck to the left. They bounced wildly over the roller coaster bumps at the beginning of the dirt road.

"Do we know where this road leads?"

"No, haven't a clue," he said, his voice harsh with tension. Shep kept both hands on the steering wheel. He couldn't race down this road. It was so pitted and torn up. "Call Preston again. Tell him where we made our turn. The closest mile marker was 54."

"Right," Maggie said, punching the numbers into the cell phone. Her heart was pounding in her chest.

While she explained their situation, Preston reviewed a map of the region.

Relief sheeted through Maggie at his response. "Preston says this road rejoins the highway about two miles down. It makes a loop."

Nodding, Shep said, "Good. Maybe the van will pass us by...."

Closing the cell phone, Maggie gripped it and the pistol. It was slow going down the muddy, bumpy road. The lights stabbed up and down with each hole they bounced into. Looking over at Shep, Maggie said, "Hunter, if we get out of this alive, I want a chance to get to know you again under less stressful circumstances. How about it?"

Giving Maggie a quick glance, he grinned a little. "That's one promise I intend to keep with you, brat." But would they survive this deadly chase? Shep couldn't promise Maggie anything.

Grimly, Maggie kept looking behind them. "I know we fight like hell. I know we're both stubborn."

"Bullheaded."

"Yes, that, too."

"I love you, anyway."

Her heart slammed into her ribs. She stared, openmouthed, at Shep's icy profile as he drove relentlessly. With each bump and shudder, glass would sprinkle into the cab from the shattered windshield.

"What?" she whispered disbelievingly. Had she heard right? Had she imagined what she had just heard?

Slowing down, Shep reached out with his right hand and gripped her left one. "I said I love you, Maggie Harper. These last twenty-four hours have proven that to me. How do you feel about it?"

His fingers were strong and warm over her cold

flesh. Gripping his hand briefly, because she knew he needed both hands on that steering wheel to keep the truck on the slippery road, she said in a choked voice, "Yes, I love you, too, Hunter. Don't ask me why. I never realized how much I missed you until you blasted back into my life."

His mouth curved into a satisfied smile. Releasing her fingers, he concentrated on driving. "Maybe what was missing before, what broke us up was my not treating you like an equal?" They had gone a mile now, and the road was curving to the right, back toward the highway.

Nodding, Maggie bowed her head momentarily. The humid, chilly wind tore through the broken windshield and made her eyes water. "Yes...that's true. Before, you treated me like a dumb bunny."

Chuckling, the sound rising up through his chest, he assured her, "No, never a dumb bunny." How badly Shep wanted to pull over, haul Maggie into his arms, kiss her senseless and make love to her. He ached to love her, to show her just how much she meant to him—and always had.

Smiling weakly, Maggie studied his hard, expressionless face in the dimness of the cab. "Do you think we'll get out of this alive?"

Shrugging, Shep slowed down and flicked off the headlights. They were within a quarter mile of the road rejoining the highway. "I'm planning on it," he told her with a growl. Maggie didn't need to know the odds right now. She was scared enough. He could see it in her blanched features. There were spots of blood here and there on her face where broken glass had struck her. It hurt him to think of her soft, firm flesh marred with those cuts. He hadn't planned on this happening. It served to tell him how dogged Black Dawn really was.

Maggie craned to see if there was any traffic on the highway ahead as they crawled cautiously forward. Unfortunately, pine trees blocked her line of vision.

"I'm getting to hate pines," she griped. "I can't see a thing to the right, Shep."

"It's okay," he soothed, and the moment the truck's tires found purchase on the asphalt, he sped up and turned toward Charleston.

Almost instantly, bullets rained around them again. To Maggie, the screech of metal, the pinging sounds, were like hailstones striking. Flinching her arms over her head, she cried out. Headlights suddenly flashed on behind them. Jerking a look over her shoulder, she yelled, "It's them!"

Damn! Shep shoved the accelerator down. "Fire back at them! Try to hit their tires. They're going to try and hit ours!"

Maggie unsnapped her seat belt. She turned around, pistol in hand, and began firing at the van racing up behind them. The headlights were on bright, blinding her. Maggie planted both her knees on the seat, her arm thrust out the broken rear window, the pistol aimed at the van. She had to steady the gun! Wind was tearing in around them. It was so cold. Icy cold. She concentrated. Bullets pinged and whined. She heard one sing past, inches from her ear. That was too close! Squeezing off shot after shot, she saw the van leap toward them.

"He's going to ram us!" she shrieked. Before she could do anything, the white van smashed into them. Maggie cried once and was thrown forward. She struck the dashboard and crumpled between it and the seat.

"Hold on!" Shep roared. He worked to keep the truck steady. Again the van slammed into them. Bullets were being fired at them from the passenger side window. More glass shattered. He felt a hot stinging on his face. Eyes riveted on the road ahead, Shep pushed the pickup to a hundred and twenty miles an hour. Gripping the wheel hard, he yelled to Maggie, "Are you hurt?"

Clambering up from her pretzel position on the floorboards, Maggie gasped, "No…" and she thrust the pistol back out the rear window and methodically began to fire once more.

Suddenly she heard another sound, like a pop. The van suddenly swerved to the right. The tires screeched.

"I hit 'em!" she shouted. She watched in amazement as the van slowed down and swerved to the right, off into the berm.

"Good," Shep exclaimed. "Now turn around here and get buckled up. We've got about ten more miles to go before we reach the police coming our way."

Her heart soaring with triumph, Maggie belted herself in. No longer were they being pursued. She'd punctured a tire on the van and rendered it useless! She felt her heart pounding like a hammer in her chest. Adrenaline was making her shaky in the aftermath of the wild, dangerous ride. "Are you okay?" she demanded, releasing the clip and putting another in its place.

"So far, so good," Shep said. He caught sight of a light to the right of them, up in the sky. "What's that?"

"What?" Maggie followed his jabbing finger. She

looked in that direction. There were red and green lights flashing above a stand of pine trees. "It's got to be a helicopter, it's so low. It must be the chopper from Parris Island!" she cried excitedly. Maggie couldn't see much in the darkness. Only when lightning from a nearby storm illuminated the night sky could she see anything. "Yes!" she shouted over the shrieking wind whistling through the cab. "It's a military helicopter for sure! It's black. All black!"

Scowling, Shep took his foot off the accelerator. "Get on the phone. Tell Preston that the helo has arrived...."

Smiling with relief, Maggie punched in the number. "Preston, this is Maggie. Hey, the helicopter from Parris Island is here!"

"What helo are you talking about? The one at the Marine Corps station is grounded. There's a thunderstorm overhead and it can't get airborne."

Puzzled, Maggie lifted her head and looked at the swiftly approaching aircraft. It was skimming the tops of the pine trees, heading straight toward them. "Shep..." she held up the cell phone "...I don't understand this. Preston says the Marine Corps helo is grounded at Parris Island due to a storm advisory. Who is this, then?"

His brows dipped immediately. "Son of a bitch, Maggie. That's *got* to be a Black Dawn aircraft! Tennyson must have been in touch with them all along!" He instantly sped up and kept his eyes on the swiftly approaching helo, which was now coming at them from the right, the side where Maggie was sitting. "Hang on!" he warned.

Confused, she gripped the door handle. "What?"

Before he could answer, Shep saw the winking of

red-and-yellow lights at the sides of the helicopter.
''Get down!'' he roared.

The scream never left Maggie's throat. She saw the
winking fireflies beneath the aircraft as it dipped directly down upon them. Maggie heard a thunk, thunk,
thunk along the earthen berm. The lights were bullets,
she realized belatedly. They were being strafed. Frozen in terror, her mind refused to operate for a second.
Shep slammed on the brakes. The truck groaned and
halted, the rear end fishtailing around. Jamming his
foot back down on the accelerator, Shep got them out
of the line of fire.

The black helicopter roared over them, less than a
hundred feet above the truck. Instantly, it banked
sharply, turned and came back at them, below the
treetops this time. The barrels of the guns fired at
them directly as Shep sped back toward the white van.

''Hold on,'' he yelled. Again he slammed on the
brakes. The truck slid sideways for a hundred feet,
then wobbled violently to a stop. Again he hit the
accelerator. The truck reared forward. Now they were
headed toward Charleston once again. The helicopter
overshot them because of his defensive driving. But
Shep knew his tactics wouldn't buy them much more
time.

''Maggie, get a fresh clip in that pistol!'' he yelled
over the screaming engine and the wind shrieking
through the broken windshield. Keeping his intense
concentration on the road, he gripped the wheel hard.
Out of the corner of his eye, he saw Maggie drop the
used clip and jam a new one into the butt of the pistol.
Good!

Before he could speak, he felt the truck shudder
drunkenly. It was being hit by fifty-millimeter am-
munition! Nothing could withstand that kind of at-

tack. Swerving and slamming on the brakes, he heard two of the tires blow simultaneously.

Maggie screamed as the truck flew out of control at the high speed. One moment they were on the highway, the next careening in wild circles off into the muddy berm and down its slope toward a stand of pines. More bullets rained up on them. Metal tore. It shrieked. She threw her hands over her face. The gravitational force of the truck turning round and round ripped at her. They were going to die! That was the last thing Maggie wanted. But she saw no way out of this. They were going to die!

The truck lurched drunkenly to a stop only a few feet from the pine trees. From overhead, the strong wash of the helicopter rotor blades buffeted them. Shep jerked off his seat belt.

"Maggie!" he roared, "get out of the truck! Get out! Now!" He knew it was only a matter of seconds before one of those gutting, fifty-millimeter bullets found the gas tank and blew them sky-high. He saw Maggie struggling with her seat belt in the darkness. Blinding light from beneath the helicopter's belly blasted in on them. There! Shep pulled her free of the belt. Reaching across Maggie, he shoved the door open. "Get out!" he cried, and pushed her with all his might.

Maggie sailed out the door. Her knees struck the embankment. The grass was wet as she landed with a thud on her hands and knees. Bullets continued to eat at the truck. Maggie looked up, terrorized, as the helicopter calmly hovered no more than a few hundred feet away, pouring hot metal into the vehicle.

Shep landed beside her. Gripping her upper arm, he jerked Maggie to her feet and pulled her toward the trees. "Run!" he roared. "Run!"

Her feet felt like concrete. She slipped a number of times on the wet grass. Shep's steadying hand kept her upright. The blast of the rotor blades, the puncturing sound, tore at her eardrums. More bullets careened into the truck. She saw Shep slow, then place himself behind her. Trying to run as hard as she could, Maggie knew he was positioning himself as a shield between her and the enemy helicopter.

She heard a whoosh. Seconds later, she felt the shock wave from the truck exploding. The huge blast knocked her off her feet and sent her tumbling to the ground. Heat followed. Rolling over and over, Maggie flailed to a stop. As she crawled to her hands and knees, her eyes huge, she saw that the truck was a mangled, fiery wreck. *Shep!* Where was he?

Maggie crawled around, searching desperately for him. She saw him fifty feet away on the ground, unmoving. *Oh, no!* Was he wounded? He'd shielded her from a blast he knew was coming. He'd done it because he loved her. Tears stung her eyes as she swayed unsteadily to her feet. Maggie lurched toward where he was lying.

Above them, the helicopter began to move—toward them. Dropping to her knees, Maggie saw Shep open his eyes. He looked confused momentarily. And then his gaze sharpened and held hers. "Shep?" She reached out shakily, touching his hard, bloody face. "Talk to me...." Maggie pleaded hoarsely. "Are you okay?"

Nodding, he forced himself to sit up. The terror in Maggie's expression made him wince. He'd never expected this. Not a Black Dawn helicopter shadowing them. It only underscored their determination to get the attaché case they believed Shep and Maggie still had. Launching himself to his feet, Shep grabbed

Maggie and dragged her against him. The noise of the helicopter as it slowly approached, hunting them, assaulted their ears. The nose lamp was moving back and forth, trying to locate them. Shep put his mouth close to Maggie's ear.

"Give me the pistol."

She held it up to him. Her hand was trembling badly.

Gripping the weapon, Shep guided Maggie to a very large pine tree. "Stay here. Whatever you do, don't run. Use this tree as cover."

Before she could ask why, Shep ran toward the helicopter, which was slowly approaching them in a methodical fashion. The high, intense beam of light swept the ground relentlessly. Sobbing for breath, Maggie wondered what Shep could do against such a powerful enemy. They'd be hunted down like dogs. A bitter taste coated her mouth.

Breathing hard, Shep zigzagged among the pine trees. The beam of light from the aircraft made it easy for him to see where he was going. He knew what Black Dawn was going to do. They would hunt them down, kill them and then land in hopes of finding the attaché case that contained the phony anthrax. Grimly, he continued to run. Well, that wasn't going to happen. He loved Maggie. And he damn well wanted a chance to love her once more—only this time, the right way—as a partner.

He hoped she would obey him now, though. She would be safer behind the thick, stout trunk of that pine. The rotor blade wash buffeted him. He was almost directly beneath the helicopter. Still not where he needed to be, Shep tried to anticipate the aircraft's next move. Running hard, he slipped and fell. With a curse, he rolled. Almost without missing a beat, Shep rolled to his feet, launched himself upright and dug his toes into the soft, muddy pine needles. He had to be at a precise spot in order to carry out his plan of attack. The pine trees were a hindrance. Would his strategy work? It *had* to!

Sobbing for breath, his lungs burning with exertion, Shep skidded to a halt. Yes, he was in perfect position! Lifting his arms, he used a nearby pine to steady his aim. Near the top of the fuselage was a red, blinking light. Every time it turned, it flashed on the rotor assembly. That was his target: the assembly. That was what he would have to try and put a bullet into. If he could do that, it would bring the helo down. Sweat ran down his face, stinging his eyes. Blinking harshly to clear his vision, he waited tensely. The tops of the pine trees were whipping violently back and forth from the rotor wash. He'd have only one chance to make the shot. Slowly, ever so slowly, the helicopter eased toward him. As the rotor appeared above the tops of the pines, Shep took aim. He'd have mere seconds to fire off the pistol at the assembly unit.

The flashing red light illuminated his target. His finger brushed the trigger as if it were a lover in need of a caress. The pistol bucked in his hands. Shep saw the bullet hit within inches of the assembly. Sparks flew. If the pilot heard the pinging sound, he'd hightail it out of there and Shep would lose his opportunity.

No way... Shep systematically pumped all eight of the bullets, one after another, into the assembly unit. He saw the bullets walking toward the rotor mechanism. Satisfaction thrummed around him. At least one would kill this machine.

Suddenly, there was a flash of light. It was followed almost instantly by the terrific thundering sound of an

explosion. The helicopter nosed up, shrieking like a
wounded being. Fire engulfed the entire rotor assembly. The aircraft sagged, then nosed down violently.
In seconds, the aircraft crashed into the thick pines
below. Shep leaped behind a tree as the wildly flailing
blades struck limbs and earth. Metal cracked and shattered, filling the air with shrieking sounds as bits of
shrapnel screamed through the darkness like lethal
scimitars, slicing through everything in their way.

The tree he crouched behind shook and shivered as
it was struck by the flying metal again and again.
Shep doubled over in a tight crouch. The entire area
shook with several more explosions—from the jet
fuel catching on fire, he knew. Peering from behind
the tree, he saw the liquid spilling like a river of fire
all around the downed aircraft. There was no way
anyone was going to survive this crash.

Standing, he realized the danger was past. Part of
the blade had lodged itself only three feet above
where he'd been crouching. When he touched the
sheared-off metal, it felt hot to his fingertips. That was
how close he'd come to death. His thoughts, his heart,
turned to Maggie. Was she safe? Had she listened to
him and stayed where he'd told her to?

Worriedly, Shep trotted toward where he'd left
Maggie. The roar of the fire continued. There was no
sense in trying to shout above it. Tucking the pistol
into his belt, he hurried forward, winding among the
trees.

Maggie looked up as someone came out of the
shadowy darkness. At first she didn't realize it was
Shep. She thought one of the Black Dawn members
had found her. The scream died in her throat when
she realized it was the man she loved, instead. With
a cry, Maggie launched herself upward and threw her

arms around Shep's neck. His arms came around her immediately, like steel bands, crushing the air from her lungs.

"You're alive!" Maggie sobbed, holding him as tightly as she could.

Placing a rough kiss on her hair, her cheek, he sought and found her mouth. Lowering her to the ground, he leaned over her, cradled her head in his large hand and guided her mouth to his.

"I love the hell out of you, Maggie Harper," he rasped, meeting her beautiful, tear-filled eyes. And he did. Now he was going to show her just how much. Their mouths clashed together, hungry, hot and needy. Just the way her body fit against his, her soft breasts pressed against his chest, her fingers digging into his massive shoulders as they deepened their kiss, was all he wanted. She tasted sweet against the specter of death that surrounded them. Her hair was damp and tangled, but he didn't care. She tasted of life in a way he'd never realized until this past twenty-four hours. He knew now he needed her for the rest of his days....

Ten

—

Maggie sighed softly as she felt the fingers of sleep easing their grasp. She didn't want to move. She felt warm and languid as she slowly came awake, became aware of the fact that Shep's arms and his body were curved around hers. Sunshine peeked in through the cracks where the hotel drapes weren't tightly drawn. Where was she? Oh, yes… As she lay there, the memories trickled back.

Shortly after the downing of the helicopter, Agent Prescott had arrived on scene. Maggie was shaken deeply by the unexpected turn of events. Never had she imagined that the aircraft would attack them from out of the sky, or that Shep would shoot it down. Life was so precious.…

She moved her fingers down the length of Shep's hairy arm. His hand was wrapped protectively across her waist. She felt very safe compared to earlier. After they both had been looked at by paramedics, Shep had demanded that Maggie be taken to Charleston, to one of the best hotels, where they could get cleaned up, shower and sleep. They were both beyond the point of exhaustion. Never had Maggie been more grateful for Shep's leadership, direction and protectiveness than at that moment. She had literally been swaying with fatigue.

A soft sigh escaped her lips now. Looking toward the clock on the bed table, she saw that it was 6:00 p.m. She'd slept a long time. How wonderful it was to have taken a hot bath after they'd arrived at the hotel. Shep had hovered nearby, ordered in some food—breakfast—while he waited for her. After he had taken a shower, they had shared the table in the suite and eaten. Food had never tasted so good after their nightmare experience with Black Dawn.

Right now, Maggie was glad to be alive. She felt the rise and fall of Shep's chest as he slept, his head nestled beside her own on the goose-down pillow. Just listening to him breathe filled her with an unparalleled joy. After last night, Maggie understood as never before how much life with Shep meant to her.

Turning over, she saw that his face was heavily bearded. He hadn't shaved last night and now he looked positively dangerous lying there, naked, at her side. She was naked, too, and she relished the thought of sharing a bed with Shep like this. They had agreed that they were simply too exhausted to do anything last night other than fall into bed and sleep in the safety of one another's arms. Sleep was healing. Sleep gave them peace from the violence that had hovered over them from the start of the mission.

Maggie moved her fingers gently through his short, dark hair, massaging the tips over his smooth, broad brow. In sleep, Shep looked far less dangerous. Normally, he was a man of action. He always would be, Maggie mused, her mouth curving softly in a smile. His lashes were thick and spiky against his ruddy cheekbones. The thick, black hair across his chest tickled and teased her breasts as she moved lithely against him. The urge to love Shep was overpowering. Maggie no longer questioned the fact that her love for him had never died. Moving her fingers in a massaging motion behind his neck, she felt the thick cords of muscle meeting his heavy, broad shoulders. There wasn't an ounce of fat on Shep. A provocative, pulsating heat pooled deeply within her body. Rising up on one elbow, she leaned over him and placed her lips against his sandpapery cheek. He smelled of the lavender soap they'd used to bathe with last night. And then there was the very male odor of him, a heady fragrance to her flaring nostrils as she inhaled deeply.

With the delicious thought of kissing Shep Hunter awake and out of the arms of sleep, Maggie eased her lips against the parted line of his mouth. She felt him come awake in an instant, a knee-jerk reaction to possible danger. Leaning back, she smiled down at him, watching as the remnants of sleep fled from his icy blue eyes and were replaced by an alert, predatory look.

"Shh...everything's okay," Maggie whispered, still smiling. She moved her fingers in a lacy pattern across his arm and over his shoulder. "We're safe.... I just woke up and decided to wake you...."

Shep gazed up at Maggie. Her red hair was in disarray and she reminded him of the wild British queen Boudicca. Her cheeks were a rosy hue, her hazel eyes simultaneously sparkling with mischief and smoky with desire. He knew that look well enough to know that she wanted him, and his body responded powerfully to her touch.

"Everything might be okay," he growled as he eased her on her back next to him, "but you aren't safe, brat."

Soft laughter gurgled up from her throat and escaped her smiling lips as Maggie settled easily next to Shep. Just the touch of his flesh, warm and dry, was evocative. As he slid one hand in a possessive motion across her right hip, she felt his strong fingers range upward across her rib cage. When he caressed the curve of her breast, Maggie sighed and closed her eyes in pleasure.

Sleep had been torn from him, but he didn't mind. He placed his weight on his left elbow as he leaned across Maggie. How beautiful and willful she looked to him. And she was here, with him. She was his. That realization made him feel strong and good as never before. As he leaned down and teased her ripening nipple with the warmth of his tongue, he felt her tense. A whisper of pleasure rippled from her. Suckling her, holding her, became his only focus. How badly he wanted to make love with her. She was his life. And last night had proven that beyond any doubt. As Shep caressed her, sucked her, he remembered starkly how he had raced back through the woods after the helicopter had fallen out of the sky like a flaming, wounded bird, to see if Maggie was still alive.

When he found her, he had needed to hold her, to reassure himself that she really *was* alive. And now, as he heard her moan with pleasure, her body arcing and sliding hotly against him, Shep savored life fully. Her fingers trailed languidly down his neck and dug deeply into his tightened shoulder muscles. She smelled of a woman's sweet fragrance laced with the clean scent of the lavender soap she'd used last night to wash the stench of their nightmare mission from her flesh.

Helplessly caught by the thudding of her wildly beating heart beneath his chest, he felt her ease her leg over his, drawing him across her. Leaning on his elbows, he kept his upper body weight off her. Opening his eyes, he drowned in the gold and green of hers. "You're so brave," he rasped as he bent down and captured her mouth.

Maggie smiled beneath his male onslaught. She felt him grind his hips, his male hardness, against her, opening her legs. She felt the gruff hair of his thighs brushing the soft firmness of hers. Moaning, she felt his maleness pushing demandingly against her moist, beckoning entrance. Without hesitation, as he took her mouth, she moved her hands down the length of his torso, settling them on his narrow hips. Guiding him, Maggie arched upward, for she wanted to claim him, to love him and welcome him deeply into her womanhood.

The instant he thrust into her, Shep groaned. His entire body trembled from the raw pleasure that she was gifting him with. He felt Maggie's slender legs wrap around his. The moment she arched shamelessly against him, he felt himself sucked into the hot, golden light of life itself. Grasping the bedsheets on either side of her head, he lifted his chin, his lips curling away from his clenched teeth. Her body was hot now, slightly damp, pulling him into a vortex of scalding heat and promise. The rocking motion of her hips increased and he was helpless to do anything other than move in the primal rhythm with her. Joy spiraled with unfettered desire as Shep lost touch with the world around them. Maggie—her scent, her soft, firm touch, the heat of her fingers raking across his tightened back muscles—was his only focus.

The hunter became the hunted. Shep felt himself spiraling completely out of control as she slid her tongue across his lower lip. Her fingers wreaked fire upon his chest, his nipples, and her hips moved in demand to take him even more deeply into herself. This was the primal Maggie he knew. In those moments just before the explosion of white-hot heat flowed out of him, he knew that he loved her with a fierceness that had never died in all those years of separation. This was the woman he wanted at his side forever.

Shep's animal groan rippled through Maggie. She tensed with him. The powerful release of her body in tandem with his made her cry out. Clutching him hard against her, she buried her face against his dampened shoulder. The pummeling crash of his heart against hers, their wild and chaotic breathing, the taste of him on her lips, all combined. She floated aimlessly, locked in his arms as they shared the greatest gift of all.

For the longest time afterward, Maggie lay in Shep's arms. She didn't want to move. She wanted to savor the satiation she felt only with him. Time meant nothing. When she finally opened her eyes, she realized the slanting sunlight had shifted and the room was gray, but she felt like a vibrant rainbow inside. Her heart sang. Her body was fulfilled as never before. Shep's fingers grazed the damp lock of hair against her brow and she gazed up at him, her eyes soft.

"I love you, did you know that?"

Shep smiled down at her, placed his mouth against her wrinkling brow and whispered, "I'd have never guessed by the way you attacked me. You always wake a sleeping man up to get what you want out of him?"

Chuckling indulgently, Maggie sighed luxuriously as he moved his fingers down the side of her face, her neck, to capture her breast. Moving her hand upward, she slid her fingers against the roughness of his jaw. "With you, yes. That's the only thing you understand—a frontal assault."

It was his turn to chuckle. Gazing down at her, Shep lost his smile. "I'm lying here beside you wondering why the hell I ever left you in the first place, brat."

"Stupid, huh? On both our parts."

"Yes," he agreed quietly. Moving his hands tenderly down her ribs, Shep captured her hip more tightly against him. They remained within one another, the intimacy strong and incredibly beautiful to him. "What I share with you now, I've never had with another woman, Maggie. Not ever."

Sobering at his honesty, Maggie realized she had never felt her femininity more strongly than in this moment. Shep was very male, but tender in his own masculine way. He knew how to be intimate with a woman; he always had. "I don't know which of us was crazier, you or me. What we share is so good, Shep. I've never experienced what I have with you with anyone else, either."

Moving his hips reflexively, he watched her eyes close with pleasure. Her lips parted. "You're so easy to love," he murmured. "You make me feel good and strong, Maggie. You always did."

Maggie gave a shuddering sigh. It was tough to talk

when he moved so provocatively within her. He knew
his power with her, and she enjoyed savoring him.
"So what are we going to do, Hunter? Keep talking
in past tense or make what we have present and future
tense?"

Grinning a little, Shep eased reluctantly from her
warm, inviting form. He didn't want to, but there
were other things to talk about. When making love to
Maggie he didn't want any interruptions. No, when
he loved her, he wanted her full, undivided attention,
and right now, he knew there were other topics that
had to be talked out between them.

He sat up, the sheet and blanket pooling around his
waist. "Come here, brat," he told her gruffly as he
leaned against the bed's antique brass headboard.
Gathering Maggie into his arms, he pulled her up beside him. She lay against him, her head nestled in the
crook of his right shoulder, her arm curved languidly
across his torso. Pulling the sheet up around her, he
shut his eyes and savored having her against him.
"Now, isn't this better?" he rumbled near her ear.
With his left hand, he moved his fingers lightly across
her small shoulder and down the smooth indentation
of her spine.

"Being with you at times like this is always better," Maggie murmured contentedly.

"So you want a present and future with me? Or
did I hear wrong?"

Opening her eyes, she gazed up at him. His icy-
blue gaze had thawed and she absorbed the warmth
that he kept so carefully closeted from the rest of the
world. Threading her fingers through the hair on his
chest, she said, "You didn't hear wrong, darling."

"I think we're mature enough to handle our dif-
ferences now, Maggie," Shep said quietly as he eased

his own fingers through the soft strands of her hair. He felt her tremble and completely relax against him. "I can see what I was doing back then. I wasn't treating you, or what you brought to the table, with respect. I always thought my way was best."

"And it isn't, not always."

"No," Shep agreed as he pressed a kiss to her cheek, "it's not." His eyes narrowed as he looked around the dim room, filled with antebellum antiques. "Last night I thought I might lose you. We survived because we worked together, as a good team should."

"You listened to me," Maggie agreed gently. "And I listened to you, too. We each brought strengths to one another, Shep. And thank goodness you listened! When you were younger, you wouldn't have."

"I know," he said miserably. He struggled with the words and the feelings. "Damn, Maggie, I feel sad. When I stop and realize my arrogance, how my know-it-all attitude kept us apart all these years... And seeing now what we have and what we missed, it makes me miserable." His hand stilled on her cheek, and Shep looked down at her. "I really screwed up. And I'm sorry. I'm not good at putting how I feel into words, brat, but I want you to know that I want a second chance with you. It will be different this time around. You're my equal. We don't need to fight and argue like we did before. I think those twenty-four hours of hell proved that we're pretty good at listening and taking direction from one another, don't you agree?"

Nodding, Maggie threaded her fingers between his. Kissing his large, skinned knuckles with small sips from her mouth, she whispered, "So, when are we going to get married, Hunter?"

That was his Maggie: bold and beautiful. A rumble of pleasure reverberated in his chest. His skin tingled where she was placing delicate, tiny kisses across his badly bruised and lacerated fingers. Did Maggie know how healing her touch was to him? He didn't think so.

"Do I have time to call my family? Could you stand getting hitched at my parents' home in Denver? Say, maybe in a week or two? It would give my other three brothers a chance, I hope, to make our wedding."

Eyes glimmering with tears, Maggie looked up at him. "Hunter, I've waited all these years for you to get your head pulled out of the sand. I don't think a couple more weeks are going to stress us out, do you? Besides, I need to call my family and tell them the good news."

His mouth pulled into a deprecating grin. "No, my redheaded woman, I don't think it will hurt anyone."

A knock on the door startled both of them. Instantly, Shep went into his mercenary mode. He slipped from the bed and reached for his pistol, which lay on the bed stand. Locking and loading it, he gestured for Maggie to remain where she was. Her eyes were wide with terror. Grimly, he went to the door, the pistol held high.

"Yes?" he called.

"Hunter? It's Preston. I need to talk with you."

Looking out the peephole in the door, Shep could see that it was the FBI agent.

"It's okay," he told Maggie. "It's Preston. Go get that hotel robe on?"

Maggie nodded and scooted out of the bed. She picked up a robe and then hurried over to him and handed him one.

"Just a minute," Shep told him through the door.

Maggie belted the thick, white terry cloth robe, pulled the covers across the bed and smoothed them out and then hurried to the windows and opened the drapes. Late evening sunlight flooded the room. Turning, she saw Shep had put the pistol away and was already in his robe and heading into the other room of the suite, which had several chairs, a couch and a coffee table. Maggie followed him.

Preston nodded in greeting as he stepped inside. "I was hoping you two were awake by now."

Shep looked down the hall both ways, then quietly shut the door behind him. "You're looking a little better around the edges, too," he told the agent.

Maggie ordered coffee from room service as the men made themselves comfortable in the living room of the suite. She closed the entrance to their bedroom and came and joined Shep on the couch opposite Preston.

"You're both looking better," the FBI agent said.

Maggie smiled and slid closer to Shep. Slipping her arm around his shoulders, she tucked her knees beneath her, content to remain close to him. "Sleep works wonders," she agreed, smiling at the agent, who was wearing a dark blue suit, a starched white shirt and red paisley tie. He looked like an FBI agent, Maggie decided. There were still dark circles beneath his eyes and the stress was still apparent in his features.

"So, what brings you to our neck of the woods?" Shep demanded. He slid his hand across Maggie's robed thigh and savored their natural intimacy.

"I had some good news I wanted to share with you," Preston said, smiling a little.

"We can use it," Maggie whispered, and traded a

smile with Shep. She saw contentment in his eyes. He was at peace, all the tension from moments ago dissolved. Absorbing his closeness, she liked the fact that his large, thick arm was draped across her lower body. Preston's eyes had widened a little at the gesture. Perhaps he didn't know of their past with one another and was astonished at their intimacy. Shep could clue him in later.

"It's about Black Dawn?" Hunter guessed.

"Yes." Preston sat up and gloated a little. "You're going to be very pleased to know that we've captured one-quarter of the entire Black Dawn contingent. What we didn't know was that six other operatives were here, waiting in Charleston, to hook up with Dr. Tennyson and his group. The people you took out when you shot down that helicopter were four in number, and were all DOA at the scene." Holding up his hands, he said, "In total, we've captured ten members of Black Dawn." He smiled even more. "And Tennyson is singing like a canary. He's agreed to spill his guts on the upper echelon of Black Dawn in exchange for immunity. He's giving us names, addresses and countries where other Black Dawn terrorists are living or hiding."

"Wonderful!" Maggie breathed. She grinned at Shep. "We're a pretty good team, aren't we?"

Just the way Maggie flushed, Shep found himself smiling in return. The triumphant look in her shining gold-and-green eyes made him go hot with longing for her all over again. He wanted to capture that smiling mouth once more. He wanted to hold her spirit, her vibrancy in his arms while he loved her.

"Yes," he admitted, "we're a damn good team."

"Couldn't have done it without you two." Preston

sobered. "Maggie, I'm sorry you got kidnapped. That was no one's fault."

"How did Tennyson get the code from you? He told me that there was a mole in the FBI feeding him the information."

"Yes, that's true. He's already given up the name of the mole," Preston told her grimly. "The man is under arrest. And he did know the codes on this mission."

"I would *never* have opened that door without the code," she told them. "I really wouldn't have."

Shep patted her leg gently. "We believe you, brat. You followed protocol."

"Well," Preston murmured, "I'm *really* sorry, Maggie. I had no idea we had a Black Dawn mole in our midst. It explains in part why we haven't, over the last couple of years, been able to trap and capture them. This agent has been feeding them information all along."

"When my brother Dev found that lab on Kauai with the help of Kulani Dawson, this whole thing broke open. It forced Black Dawn's hand," Shep said.

"No doubt about it," Preston agreed. "If it hadn't been for Morgan Trayhern, or Perseus, we would never have cracked this case. It goes to show us how private enterprises like Perseus are worth bringing in under the government tent. I'm glad Morgan works *with* us. He has incredible people."

Maggie brushed her fingers delicately against Shep's thick, corded neck. "Yes, he has incredible people who are completely committed to him," she agreed.

Preston cleared his throat. Rising, he adjusted the knotted tie at his throat. "Well, I've got to get back to the Charleston office. You have our thanks." He shook their hands. "I'll be talking to Morgan, too. Dr. Harper, your heroism may never be known publicly, but for what it's worth, I think you're one of the most courageous women I've ever run across."

Maggie flushed beneath the agent's sincere praise. "Thanks, Agent Preston."

"I know," Shep growled, "and that's enough."

"I'll let myself out. You two enjoy the night and get some rest."

"Couldn't you stay and at least have coffee with us? I've got it ordered," Maggie offered.

Preston smiled tiredly. "I'd like to, but I have to get back to the office. Thanks anyway. You two enjoy a well-deserved quiet evening together."

As the door quickly closed, Maggie turned her attention back to Shep. "How about that? A happy ending."

Shep patted her calf and slid his fingers around her dainty foot. "A partial victory," he warned her. "Terrorist groups will always exist. In this case, it sounds like we chopped off the head of the snake. Black Dawn may be gone, but that doesn't mean there aren't other factions out there waiting to take its place."

"Humph," Maggie said, her skin tingling where Shep touched her, "no rest for the wicked?"

Shrugging, he released her foot and slid his arms around her. He maneuvered Maggie across his lap so that she lay against him, her arms resting languidly around his shoulders. "Right now, my world, my existence, is centered on one red-haired lady. Black Dawn is crippled. We did some good work. The world is safe for a while, at least." Gazing into her sparkling eyes, he whispered, "I love you, Maggie Harper. And I'm going to keep loving you with a fierceness that will last until we draw our last breaths.''

Framing his face, she smiled brokenly. Shep was a man of few words and she knew the gift he'd just given her. ''You're one of a kind, darling. My kind.''

''Even if we fight like cats and dogs?''

''Oh, I'm sure we'll have our moments.'' Maggie laughed gently. Moving her fingers tenderly across his flesh, she watched his eyes burn that darker blue color that warned her of how much he desired and loved her. It sent a wonderful tingly sensation up and down her spine.

''Partners can disagree without hurting one another with words and actions,'' Shep promised her.

''And we'll both give each other the respect and the space we need when we hit those bumps in the road, Shep. I know we will.''

Sighing, he said, ''I've been too long without you, brat. And if this mission did nothing but point that out, then that's enough.''

Smiling tenderly, Maggie leaned over and grazed his mouth with her lips. ''You're *more* than enough for me, Shep Hunter. The war between us is over. We're going to spend the rest of our lives learning peaceful coexistence with one another.''

Moving his mouth against the sweet softness of her lips, he rasped, ''And I'm going to enjoy learning from you, sweet woman of mine....''

* * * * *

Read the stories where
MORGAN'S MERCENARIES
*began! Coming in May 2000
from Silhouette Books,*

LOVE AND GLORY

*This special three-in-one volume features
the Trayherns—a family bound by
honor…and destined to find love.
Meet Noah Trayhern in*

A QUESTION OF HONOR

Discover Alyssa Trayhern in

NO SURRENDER

*And read the story of how
Morgan Trayhern meets his
beloved Laura in*

RETURN OF A HERO.

*Three action-packed stories of love
and adventure—one fabulous
Lindsay McKenna book!*

*Turn the page for a sneak preview
of Morgan's story,*

RETURN OF A HERO…

For the first time, Laura detected an opening in the wall that so thoroughly protected Morgan. As he sat across the table from her drinking coffee, she felt comfortable talking to him. "When I first came here after graduating from college, I rented this house." She gestured around the room with her hand. "I fell in love with it. At the time my dad was over in Vietnam, and I sent him pictures of every room." Her voice grew warm with love. "He was so excited for me. We traded letters for six months on how I was going to decorate each room." She picked up her cup, sipping the cooling coffee. "I think my letters and dreams for this house helped my dad. It was a piece of reality from a world other than the one he fought in daily." Laura shook her head. "I still have all his letters...."

A lump formed in Morgan's throat. "Letters from

home meant everything to me—'' He caught himself. Damn!

"You were in Vietnam?'' Of course, he would have been the right age.

A frown furrowed his brow. "Yeah, I was over there.'' The words came out harsh and clipped.

Biding time because she heard his anger and pain, Laura drank her coffee. She'd met many veterans who didn't want to discuss what had happened to them over there, and she felt Morgan was like that, too. Gently, she steered the conversation back to her father. "The living room was Dad's idea—the colors and the fabric. And so was the kitchen.'' Fondly, she laughed. "At the time we were playing this silly game. I really didn't have any money for redecorating. But that didn't matter. At least it offered Dad some sanity while he was over there. And Mom didn't worry as much, because she had something to do, too.''

Morgan could no longer sit still. The ghosts were rising in his memory again—the anger and the frustration along with them. He paced slowly around the kitchen. "So how did you manage to get this house bought and decorated?''

"Dad was killed in a rocket attack in the seventh month of his tour. What I didn't realize was that he'd taken out nearly half a million dollars in insurance before he left for Vietnam, just in case he did get killed.'' She rose, picking up her cup and saucer, and moved carefully to the drainboard. "So I bought this house and Mom and I took each room, just as we'd planned in our letters to Dad, and decorated. This home reflects the love we had as a family. That's why I love it so much.''

Morgan tried to fight his need to hold her, but he walked up to her. Gently placing his hands on her shoulders, he looked down at her. "You're like this home," he told her, his voice rough with emotion, "warm, caring and beautiful."

It felt so natural to lean her head against his chest and rest for a moment. Laura sighed as Morgan's arms slid around her shoulders, drawing her gently against him. "Right now, I don't feel very strong, Morgan."

She fitted against his tall frame, Morgan thought, a willow in comparison to an oak. The fragrance that was hers alone filled his nostrils. He fought to keep his touch light and comforting, not intimate, as he wanted. "You're stronger than you think," he told Laura gruffly, his mouth near her ear. Caressing her back with his hands, he felt the firm softness of her flesh beneath the silk blouse. If he didn't step back, he'd kiss her, and that wouldn't be right.

Laura felt bereft as Morgan gently disengaged himself. "I—I'm sorry. I shouldn't have—"

"Shh," Morgan remonstrated, keeping one hand on her upper arm as she swayed. "That's one of many things I like about you, Laura Bennett—your ability to show your feelings. If you're feeling weak, you lean. If you're feeling strong, you get feisty." He grinned. "You're one hell of a woman, did you know that?"

She shook her head, forcing herself to retreat from him. Shaken by the unexpected contact, Laura found herself wanting more. "No, you're wrong," she whispered, her voice strained, "you're the one who's special."

Snorting vehemently, Morgan got busy and cleared

the rest of the dishes from the table. "I'm special all right," he growled. *Just ask the press or the Pentagon. They'll tell you all about me.* He glanced at her after setting the dishes in the sink. Her lips were pursed, as if she were deep in thought. All this seemed like a fevered dream. This house that throbbed with life, the beauty and generosity of Laura, were all baubles being dangled cruelly in front of him and his harsh existence. If she found out he was Morgan Trayhern, the traitor, she'd scorn him. Sadness flowed through him, effectively squelching the fires of longing for her. Morgan hadn't fully realized just how tough it would be to stay around Laura. Somehow he'd have to contain his unraveling emotions. Maybe by tonight things would settle into a routine, and he'd be able to control the feelings that Laura brought to brilliant, yearning life within him. Maybe...

Don't miss Silhouette's newest cross-line promotion,

Four royal sisters find their own Prince Charmings as they embark on separate journeys to find their missing brother, the Crown Prince!

The search begins
in October 1999 and
continues through February 2000:

On sale October 1999: **A ROYAL BABY ON THE WAY**
by award-winning author **Susan Mallery** (Special Edition)

On sale November 1999: **UNDERCOVER PRINCESS**
by bestselling author **Suzanne Brockmann** (Intimate Moments)

On sale December 1999: **THE PRINCESS'S WHITE KNIGHT**
by popular author **Carla Cassidy** (Romance)

On sale January 2000: **THE PREGNANT PRINCESS**
by rising star **Anne Marie Winston** (Desire)

On sale February 2000: **MAN...MERCENARY...MONARCH**
by top-notch talent **Joan Elliott Pickart** (Special Edition)

ROYALLY WED
Only in—
SILHOUETTE BOOKS

Available at your favorite retail outlet.

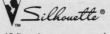

Visit us at www.romance.net

SSERW

If you enjoyed what you just read,
then we've got an offer you can't resist!

Take 2 bestselling love stories FREE!

Plus get a FREE surprise gift!

Clip this page and mail it to Silhouette Reader Service™

IN U.S.A.	IN CANADA
3010 Walden Ave.	P.O. Box 609
P.O. Box 1867	Fort Erie, Ontario
Buffalo, N.Y. 14240-1867	L2A 5X3

YES! Please send me 2 free Silhouette Desire® novels and my free surprise gift. Then send me 6 brand-new novels every month, which I will receive months before they're available in stores. In the U.S.A., bill me at the bargain price of $3.12 plus 25¢ delivery per book and applicable sales tax, if any*. In Canada, bill me at the bargain price of $3.49 plus 25¢ delivery per book and applicable taxes**. That's the complete price and a savings of over 10% off the cover prices—what a great deal! I understand that accepting the 2 free books and gift places me under no obligation ever to buy any books. I can always return a shipment and cancel at any time. Even if I never buy another book from Silhouette, the 2 free books and gift are mine to keep forever. So why not take us up on our invitation. You'll be glad you did!

225 SEN CNFA
326 SEN CNFC

Name	(PLEASE PRINT)	
Address	Apt.#	
City	State/Prov.	Zip/Postal Code

* Terms and prices subject to change without notice. Sales tax applicable in N.Y.
** Canadian residents will be charged applicable provincial taxes and GST.
  All orders subject to approval. Offer limited to one per household.
  ® are registered trademarks of Harlequin Enterprises Limited.

DES99   ©1998 Harlequin Enterprises Limited